WOMEN RISING

MAE ANDREWS

Women Rising

Mae Andrews

CREATIVE
ENDEAVORS

Creative Endeavors, LLC, Smithsburg MD

Table of Contents

Author's Note

The stories were organized chronologically to bring you from the past, around the 1990s, into the present and future. However, if you would rather skip around and read each character's story, you do that. This book is about agency and decisions, including how you chose to read it.

Life is a mosaic of emotions that don't flow smoothly and transition gently. The shifts between stories might be jarring. That being said, the contents of this book may also be triggering and disturbing to some readers. Please take warning that the content is for adults only. This book is not to be used as a resource for legal advice or sexual education.

Content Warnings (may also contain spoilers):

Sexual assault, sexual assault of a minor, rape, rape of a minor, dubcon, coercive control, intimate partner abuse, explicit sex scenes, explicit language, anal sex, oral sex, divorce, anxiety attack.

But these characters are really fucking resilient.

Acknowledgments

To my son for giving me the time and space to write and learn. Your existence has made me a better person.

To my friend of thirty plus years for reading it. Your support through everything is invaluable.

To the man that listened to me talk about it. You were a source of inspiration.

To for the tools, resources, and classes. I had no idea how much I needed to learn.

To you the reader for taking a chance. The book falls into the void without you.

Annie: Age 10

In the spring, the apple tree in front of Annie's house was soft shades of pink and white. Whenever the wind blew, the scent of apple blossoms drifted through the air. Bird feeders hung from the branches. Cardinals, blue jays, and chickadees could always be spotted close by. Wind chimes of all sizes swayed in the breeze. There was a small orchestra of bright and cheery clinks, deep and brassy bongs, and wooden plunks with every breeze. The tree was large with a small fort in it where Annie would read. Other times, a friend joined her. They talked about the boys they liked or the fears heavy on their minds. Sometimes, they created a fantastical story incorporating whatever books or movies they were interested in.

As spring progressed, the wind carried the blossoms with it. They floated through the air like sailboats. The front lawn would be decorated with tiny pink and white flowers. Come summer, the tree would be covered with wild apples too tart to eat. The tree in the backyard had better-tasting fruit. Strangely, the blossoms weren't as beautiful and the smell not as sweet. The tree was smaller as well, which made collecting the fruit easier. It always surprised Annie that those apples tasted better.

Apple trees in autumn weren't as colorful as the rest of the foliage. In fact, the ripe apples in the front would fall and create a mushy, dangerous mess. Annie distinctly remembered walking beneath the tree and having them roll under her feet like skates. The next thing she knew, her butt was on the ground and her clothing splattered with mashed, rotten apples. She needed to be mindful of the bees that darted around, too. The deer loved those apples. In the quiet of the early morning and evening, deer would come down from the woods and snack on the feast lying on the yard.

Annie would gather the apples in the back, choosing the larger fruit that didn't appear to have any worms. She checked the ground and collected the half-bruised ones as well. Sometimes, she'd grab an apple too small or green and throw it to knock better fruit off the higher part of the tree. It took a lot of apples to make anything, but every autumn there was enough for a pie.

She would sit with her mom at the table and help peel and slice them. They were thrown in a bowl to be decorated with cinnamon, sugar, and flour. Annie's mom made the crust from scratch and would place it in a red ceramic dish. Annie would fill it up with the pie filling and carefully place the crust on top. She looked forward to this every autumn.

Upstate New York had long, hard winters that left her favorite tree barren. The wooden limbs twisted and turned. Her fort held a pile of snow, and branches would break under the weight. After the dark months, the little specks of green leaves in the early spring would bring her great joy. It broke up the brown and gray of the muddy ground, bare trees, and small piles of dirty snow. Spring was by far her favorite season.

Sylvia and Beth: Ages 12 and 13

"Sylvia! Phone!" Mark's voice yelled out.

"Coming!" Sylvia flew out of her room and grabbed the phone from her brother's hand. She stretched the cord down the hall into the bathroom and closed the door. Her mom had bought a new phone cord not long ago. However, Sylvia was stretching it out so it could reach her room. She had several more feet to go before she reached that goal. "Hello?"

"Sylvie! Do you want to go to the homecoming football game with me? Ryan asked me to come! I can't tell my parents that, but you can come with me and spend the night after." Beth, Sylvia's best friend, rapidly spoke in one breath.

"Uh, yeah! Of course I want to! He asked you to go with him? I can't believe it! You're going to the game with a freshman!"

"You are too! He said some of his teammates are going to be there."

"We are going to be hanging out with the basketball team! Is he getting his license when he turns sixteen?"

"Yeah. He said his dad already bought him a car."

"I can't wait! Maybe he will take you to the movies when he starts driving!"

"Well, he hasn't asked me out yet. I'm hoping he will soon."

"Maybe at the game!"

"I hope so. He was one of the guys nominated for homecoming king for the freshman class. He asked me to go to the dance, too. I really want him to ask me out. Ask your mom if you can spend the night."

"Mom's not here. She won't be home until later tonight. I'll tell Mark, and he can tell her. Or I'll write her a note. She won't care. I'll be with you. Wait." Sylvia paused.

"What?"

"Shhhh!!!! I heard something." Several long seconds of silence followed. "Mark! Mark, get off the other phone! Stop listening in on my conversation!"

"You're going to the game with the basketball team? They are three years older than you!" he scolded into the receiver.

"I'm going with Beth, and a few of the guys will be there. I'm not going with the *entire* team.   Stop   being dramatic and stop eavesdropping on my calls!"

"You are gonna freeze. It's supposed to be cold tonight. Since when did you want to be popular?"

"I want to be with Beth! Just tell Mom where I'm going. And get off the phone!"

Mark grumbled, and a click followed.

"Oh my God, Sylvia. How could you tell he was on the other line? I couldn't hear anything."

"I can tell. It sounds a little different. Mom wanted a phone in the kitchen so she could sit at the table. I think she could have stretched the cord out to reach there. It's not like this is a huge apartment. I'm gonna pack my bag and walk over. I'll see you soon!"

"Okay! See you soon!"

Sylvia went to her room, grabbed her old bookbag and started packing. Her brother was right about one thing. It had been getting cold when the sun went down. She threw her dark brown hair into a ponytail and slipped on her combat boots. Her plaid long-sleeve button-up went over her t-shirt, and she threw a jean jacket on top. She scribbled a message on a piece of mail lying on the kitchen table. "Mark! I'm leaving."

"You aren't gonna tell me what's going on?"

"You were eavesdropping! You already heard! I'll be back tomorrow. I left a note, but tell Mom for me, too. Okay?"

"I don't like you going with boys that are fifteen and sixteen."

"They are in your grade. Don't you know them?"

"Yeah. That's why I don't want you with them. The guys on the basketball team are assholes."

"It's the homecoming game. There will be tons of people! I'll be fine. Just because you're a loner doesn't mean I have to be. You are probably a jerk to them, and that's why they are assholes to you." Sylvia walked out of the house, slamming the door behind her.

After a thirty-minute walk, she arrived at Beth's house and knocked on the door. She waited, then tried again. Her house was large, so it always took a while for someone to answer the door. Beth answered on the third knock. "I'm almost ready! I'll be in my room finishing up."

"I'll be right there." Sylvia took off her boots as her friend ran upstairs. She detoured to the kitchen, grabbed a drink and a snack, and joined her in her room. "Can I live with you? You have so much space! You have the best snacks! I can stay in the guest room."

She laughed. "You could. We don't use it. I'm almost done with my makeup. My dad is still at the office, and my mom went grocery shopping. If we leave soon, they won't see me wearing it. We'll have to sneak back after the game so I can wash it off."

"Do you think we can cut through the park to go to the school?"

"Definitely!"

Beth finished putting on frosty pink eye shadow, matching lip gloss, and glitter lotion. Her blue eyes sparkled with excitement as she curled small strands of blonde hair on the sides of her face. She threw on her bubble coat and put her earmuffs in her pocket before walking out the door.

The girls chatted about classes that day as they walked to the park. Around the edges were patches of trees people referred to as 'the woods'. There was a shortcut that led to the neighborhood by the school. It was a clear, worn path used by adults and students. Sylvia loved the park itself, along with the woods surrounding it and the small creek running through it. It was about four feet wide and easily crossed by stepping on stones. However, the recent rain had elevated the water level. Sylvia jumped from rock to rock down the middle of the creek as Beth walked on the bank.

"When I am older, I'm buying a house in the woods." Sylvia said. "It will be a big house, like yours. Not a tiny apartment like mine. I'll have the whole place to myself."

"Won't you be lonely?"

"No. I can't wait to have my own space. When my dad left and we had to move, I had to give a lot of my stuff away because it wouldn't fit in the new place. It's cramped with the three of us. Now, Mark thinks he's my father. Mom got a second part-time job on top of her full-time one a few months ago. She's gone all the time, and that made my brother worse. The only thing helping right now is that he started a job. He and Mom are trying to save up enough money to buy him a car when he's sixteen."

"Sometimes, I'm lonely. It's a big house. Dad is always at work. Mom is always busy doing something."

"What does she do?"

"I don't know. Stuff in the community. PTA."

"At least she takes you to your practices and games. I'm hoping Mark will drive me places when he gets his license. I'm tired of walking everywhere."

"Yeah. I do like that. She is always at my games, but she's volunteering. I don't think she pays attention to me when I play."

"My mom is always working. She tries to make a couple of games. She always wants me to share with her about how it went when she can't go." Sylvia stopped traipsing down the center of the creek as they reached the main path through the woods. Beth hopped across the rocks to join her. "Did you know there are rivers that you can raft on?" Sylvia asked. "One day, Beth, I'm going to raft down a raging river. I'm going to climb the side of a mountain and zipline through a rainforest."

"You are crazy, Sylvie!"

Conversation bounced from subject to subject as the girls made their way to the school. Outside the gates of the football field, Ryan was standing and talking to three boys and a girl. They recognized the boys from the basketball team. One was holding hands with the girl they didn't know.

"Beth! His friends are cute!"

She laughed. "Maybe you will start dating one! We could double date together!"

"My brother would kill me. He says I'm twelve and don't need to be hanging out with fifteen- and sixteen-year-old guys."

"Well, I'm older than you. It's okay for me."

"By six months!"

"I'm thirteen and Ryan is only two years older. That's better than three years."

"No. No, I don't want to date anyone. I just want to look at them." The girls laughed.

As they approached the group, Ryan smiled. Beth stood next to him, and he wrapped his arm around her. "Beth, that's Chris, Dylan, James, and his girlfriend Rachel. Come on. Let's grab a seat before it fills up."

Sylvia trailed behind the small pack. Beth glanced over her shoulder, scanning to find her. When she did, they locked eyes, and Beth raised her eyebrows, silently asking if she was okay. Sylvia smiled and nodded, and her friend grinned back. The group laughed and joked as they made their way through the bleachers. Ryan pulled Beth towards the center near midfield. James and Rachel followed. Chris and Dylan sat behind them on the next row up. Sylvia took a seat next to Dylan and above Beth. Most of Beth's focus stayed on Ryan and whomever he was speaking to. The boys talked about teachers and students Sylvia didn't know and cracked jokes she didn't understand. She could tell their stories originated from other times they hung out together. She sat quietly with her hands in her pockets, trying to eavesdrop. The conversation with her brother replayed in her head and made her more self-conscious.

Once the game started, she could tell it was going to be a tight match. When her dad lived with them, he was an avid football fan. They grew up watching football, and Mark still did when his team was on. Sylvia decided she would focus on Beth and the game. Dylan and Chris seemed to love the sport as well. They had conversations among themselves about the plays and intermittently interrupted discussions that Ryan, James, and Rachel were having. Sylvia couldn't help herself. She listened in on their banter, making her own comments. After a couple of interjections, Dylan looked at her. "I'm Dylan. That's Chris. We didn't catch your name."

"Sylvia."

"You're a friend of Ryan's girl, right?"

"Yeah. I'm Beth's friend."

"You like football, Sylvia?" Chris leaned around Dylan. "Who's your team?"

"I don't have one, but my brother watches the Patriots. Who's yours?"

"Cowboys." Dylan smiled.

"Both of you?"

"Yep," Chris gleefully said.

"This is going to be a long game then." She rolled

her eyes in mock annoyance, and the boys laughed. Sylvia turned her attention to Beth. Ryan's arm was still around her, pulling her close. She was starting to join in the conversation, leaning into Ryan, smiling bigger and laughing more. Her natural bubbly personality was starting to come through. Towards the end of the first quarter, Chris and Dylan left. When they came back, each of them had soda, a burger, and fries. Dylan sat back in his previous seat. Chris moved to the other side of Sylvia.

"Sylvie, my mom gave me money for food when you are ready to eat something." Beth said over her shoulder.

"I'm okay right now."

Now that Sylvia was in the middle, she was pulled into Chris and Dylan's discussions. As they made her laugh, she became more relaxed. They included Beth as well. Sylvia noticed Ryan's face when they spoke to her. His eyes narrowed, and his arm gripped Beth possessively. When he became distracted by James and Rachel, his arm would loosen. Chris and Dylan would pull Beth's attention back to them, and Ryan's arm would tighten. Beth beamed up at him. Sylvia intently studied them. Ryan didn't like his friends talking to Beth. Beth was enjoying Ryan holding her tight. Sylvia tried to tell herself that if her friend was okay with it, she should be as well. It wasn't working.

By the end of the second half, Sylvia's breath was forming tiny clouds in front of her face. She wished she had grabbed a hat and gloves. Chris and Dylan were very animated as they talked to each other. They leaned over Sylvia and had slowly moved closer together. It didn't help that it was a packed game without a lot of space on the bleachers, which squeezed their group tighter. Chris and Dylan's legs pressed against hers, keeping her a little warmer in those spots. Mark's voice stayed in her head. She kept watching for signs that they were assholes, but so far they had been friendly. Secretly, she was enjoying the attention. Ryan, James, and Rachel weren't talking to her, but James wasn't talking to Beth either. Sylvia tucked her hands inside her jacket and long sleeve shirt, wishing for something warm to drink.

"Beth, wanna get something from the concession stand?"

Dylan turned toward her. "Don't go now. It's a terrible time. Everyone is in line since it's halftime and they don't want to miss the game. You'll be stuck standing forever. Wait until halfway through the third quarter."

Sylvia looked around. The concession stand wasn't visible from her seat, but the crowd in the stands had thinned out. Chris and Dylan remained sitting close to her.

"They run out of the good stuff after halftime." Chris added. "What do you want?"

"Hot cocoa."

"Oh, you should be fine with that. Were you gonna get anything?" Chris said to Beth.

"I don't know. I'll see what's left."

"I'll buy something for you. Don't worry." Ryan said. She gazed up at him, smiling.

As the game restarted, the bleachers filled up. Sylvia was having a great time with Chris and Dylan, despite being cold and hungry. The game stayed close and exciting. It was 14-17 with her team trailing. Beth turned to her about halfway through the third quarter. "Come with me. I have to go to the bathroom. We can go to the concession stand, too. I'm hungry."

"Me too!" Sylvia stood up to leave. Beth followed, but so did Ryan.

"I'll take her to the bathroom inside the school. There's a side door that's unlocked most of the time. We can bring you something when we come back."

"I'll still go with you. I want to warm up, and my legs are hurting from sitting."

"Wait here. We won't be long. I'll take her."

Sylvia didn't sit down. She was about to insist again when Beth spoke. "It's okay, Sylvie. Stay here and enjoy the game. You like football. I'll bring you back cocoa and something to eat."

Sylvia was torn. She did want to hang out with Chris and Dylan and watch the game. She also wanted to go with her friend, move around and warm up. She decided Beth was more important and kept standing.

"Sylvie! I'll be right back. Watch the game."

Reluctantly, she sat down. Ryan slid his hand in Beth's, leading her through the people and bleachers. James and Rachel stayed, but were slightly removed from the group. Chris and Dylan tried to reassure and distract Sylvia. A few minutes later, the home team made a key first down, and the crowd went wild. Tension was in the air as the away team called a timeout, and it didn't lift as the teams walked back on the field. The quarterback's first pass was incomplete. On the second down, he threw the ball to a receiver who was tightly covered. She held her breath, nervous that it was going to be intercepted. It fell right in the receiver's hands, and he took off running, scoring a touchdown. Her school took the lead for the first time. Chris, Dylan, and Sylvia jumped up, screaming and cheering. The excitement and movement helped warm her up for a moment, but after sitting back down her teeth started to chatter.

Dylan looked at her, then at the scoreboard. "Man. Where are they? I thought they'd be back by now. It's almost the fourth quarter."

"There might be a line at the concession stand." Sylvia answered.

"I'm hungry again, anyway. I'll check if they are waiting." Dylan stood up to leave.

"I'm hungry, too. I'll come with you." Chris followed.

Sylvia stood. "Beth is my friend. I'm going too."

"Sylvie, you have to save our seats. We'll be right back, okay?" Dylan dug his hands into his pockets. "You are freezing. Put the gloves on."

"Here." Chris took off his hat and placed it on Sylvia's head, then pulled his hood up. "Wear that, too. Save our spots." They turned around and left.

Sylvia sat down, but couldn't pay attention to the game with everyone gone. It didn't take long for someone to try to sit in their area. Where seven people had been, now there were three, appearing like vacancies in the bleachers. Sylvia stopped two sets of people from sitting in the space. Chris and Dylan returned shortly after.

"The line wasn't long, but we didn't see them. There also wasn't much food left." Dylan gave her a Styrofoam cup. "Here, Sylvie. You wanted hot cocoa."

"They did have fries. That was about it. I got you some." Chris held a side of fries in each hand and handed her one. "They'll probably be back soon."

Sylvia smiled as she took the gifts, and Chris and Dylan sat down close to her. The hat, gloves, hot food and drink, and their legs against hers started to warm her up. She stopped shivering. The game was still close at 21-17. It appeared the home team had rallied and their defense was shutting everything down, but Sylvia had a hard time paying attention. The clock on the scoreboard ticked down as Beth still didn't come back. Halfway through the fourth quarter, Ryan and Beth came into sight. Ryan was holding her hand and leading her through the crowd. Beth was looking down as he led her. She wasn't smiling.

"What the fuck, man?" Dylan said to Ryan as he sat in front of them. "Where the hell did you guys go?"

"The door is on the other side of the school. It's a walk. We had to dodge a janitor, too. We weren't supposed to be in the building."

"Why didn't you take her to the same bathroom everyone else is using?" Chris asked.

"It's warmer inside. I wanted to warm up. So did she."

Sylvia eyed her friend. "Beth, did you eat something?"

"Everything was out." Ryan answered.

"Dude, we just ordered fries." Dylan responded. "And hot cocoa."

"We just came from there. They were out." Ryan snapped.

"Well, the game is almost over." Chris said. "You missed a hell of a play."

"Oh shit! We are winning!" Ryan exclaimed, his eyes on the scoreboard.

Chris and Dylan started updating Ryan on what had happened while he was gone. Sylvia stared at her friend. Beth's eyes met hers, and she smiled in an attempt to reassure her. Then her eyes flicked down. Ryan's arm was wrapped around her again, gripping her. Beth wasn't looking at him, and she wasn't smiling anymore. No one else noticed. The atmosphere in the stadium remained excited. The game was almost over, and her school's defense held. The crowd erupted again when the visiting team's quarterback was sacked. They tried to go for a conversion on fourth down, but it failed. Although the home team didn't score again, it was clear they were going to win. The end of the game resulted in everyone going wild. Dylan and Chris were screaming. Sylvia yelled with feigned enthusiasm. She had been celebrating with them almost the entire time and didn't want to bring attention to her altered mood. She was going to pretend to be excited.

Getting out of the bleachers was a slow process. With Dylan in front of her and Chris behind her, they helped push her through the swarm of people. Beth and Ryan trailed far behind. Sylvia kept looking back and bumping into Chris. He leaned close to her ear. "We have a meeting spot outside the gate. Don't worry." She nodded.

James and Rachel made it out first. Dylan and Chris led Sylvia over to them to wait.

"You should come to one of our basketball games, Sylvie." Chris said.

"Yeah. It'll be a lot warmer." Dylan added, "And I bet Beth will want to come for Ryan".

"I'm not sure. I'm hoping to join the swim team in the winter, but I should be able to catch a game."

Ryan and Beth joined the group. "My dad will be here soon. We can drive you home," Ryan offered.

"No. We walked," Sylvia answered. "We are walking home."

"Sylvie, it's cold as fuck out here." Dylan said. "Ryan's dad can take the two of you."

"No. We are walking home."

"You can walk." Ryan said. "Beth can ride with me."

"No." Sylvia's voice became loud. "You already took her from me. You had her all game. We walked here, and we are walking back."

"Jealous much?" Ryan smirked, his mouth curling in a snide smile.

"Ryan, don't be an ass," Chris said. "Sylvie. It's cold and dark. How long will it take to walk home?"

"Not long. We go through the park."

"Don't go through the woods at night." Dylan said.

"Fine. We won't. But we are walking."

Chris turned to Dylan. "How did we not notice how stubborn she is?"

"Should have guessed. Any girl who likes football like she does has to have a backbone."

Sylvia moved to grab Beth's hand. Ryan pulled her away. "Why don't you let me ask my girlfriend what she wants to do?" He turned to her. "Baby, do you want my dad to drive you home?"

Beth looked at him with a small smile but cut her eyes to Sylvia. Her eyes darted back and forth again. "I'll walk with Sylvie. We'll be okay. Thank you though."

"Call me when you're home. You have my number, right?" She nodded, and he kissed her lips. When Beth's back turned, he glared at Sylvia.

Sylvia glared back. She slid her hand into Beth's and dragged her away.

"Bye Sylvie." Dylan called from behind her.

Sylvia peered back and smiled as she walked away. "Bye Dylan! Bye Chris! Oh! Your hat and gloves."

"Keep them." Chris said. "You're walking. You will need them."

"Yeah, it's fine." Dylan agreed.

Sylvia and Beth were quiet for a long time. They didn't cut through the woods or the park, exactly as Sylvia promised. They kept to the sidewalks and areas with streetlights. Sylvia knew this area well, but hadn't been out this late before. It was cold. Their hands were icy, even Sylvia's with the gloves on. Their teeth chattered and their breath came out in small clouds with every exhale.

"They called you Sylvie, huh?" Beth smiled, breaking the silence. "And you got a hat and gloves. And cocoa and fries."

Sylvia grinned. "Chris and Dylan were sweet."

"Do you like one of them more? Would you want to go out with one of them?"

"No. I like them both, but I couldn't date both. So I don't want to date either of them."

Beth laughed. "What would your brother say if you had two boyfriends?"

"Oh my god! Mark would flip out! It would be worse if he knew how old they were. He would give one boyfriend a hard time. His head would explode if I had two. I don't think my mom would like that either. I'd be a slut." Sylvia paused. "Ryan asked you to be his girlfriend?"

"I guess he did."

"You guess he did?"

"Well, he said I was his girlfriend just now."

"Did he ask?"

"No. He said I was."

Silence fell over them. They dropped hands and shoved them into their pockets. "Why were you gone so long?" Sylvia glanced at her friend, who stared at the ground quietly. She didn't recognize her facial expression.

"I mean, you had two boys keep you company." Beth lips twitched up in a half smile.

"Beth, I'm being serious. Why were you gone so long? Did you even eat?"

"I'm not hungry."

"But you were hungry."

"I was. I'm not now though." She stared at the sidewalk. "Like Ryan said, the side door was far away. We didn't want the janitor to find us inside the school. That's all." Silence followed.

"Will we still be able to sneak in so your parents don't notice you're wearing makeup?" Sylvia broke the silence, trying to pull Beth from wherever her mind was dragging her.

"Oh yeah. It won't be hard. If my mom is downstairs, you may have to distract her. I want to take a shower. I can wash it off then."

"Okay. I'll distract her in the kitchen. I do that all the time."

Beth smiled, a genuine one that reached her eyes. Sylvia saw the 'thank you' they held.

No one was downstairs when they came in. Sylvia changed into pajamas and Beth vanished to the bathroom. While she showered, Sylvia went to the kitchen and made cocoa and something for them to eat. Beth's mom appeared and asked about the game. Sylvia had to ramble and exaggerate the story since Beth took longer than she thought she would. When she finally came down, she was wearing pajamas and carrying a pillow and blanket. Beth told her mom they were going to put a movie on and sleep in the living room. Her mom half-heartedly attempted conversation. Beth gave vague and generic answers, attempting to be upbeat. Her mom didn't stay long once her daughter was there, wished them goodnight, and went upstairs to bed.

"Can we watch Carrie tonight?" Beth asked.

"Sure. I'm gonna grab a pillow and blanket from the guest room and bring it down. I made you something to eat. You should eat something Beth."

"Thanks Sylvie."

Beth stretched out on the couch while Sylvia curled up in the reclining chair. They fell asleep before the movie was over. The next day the girls hung out watching TV. Sylvia could tell something still wasn't right with her friend, but didn't say anything else. It was early afternoon when she headed home. Mark was in the living room when she walked into the apartment.

"Is Mom here?"

"No. She left for her other job a couple hours ago. She said she would be home about four. Did you freeze?"

"Oh my god it was so cold!"

"Even after you got the hat and gloves?"

Sylvia's head whipped around. She glared at her brother. "Were you spying on me?"

"No."

"Did you go to the game?"

"Yeah. Kenny asked me if I wanted to go with him. It was a good game."

"You went to spy on me!"

"I went because Kenny asked me." He paused. "Dylan and Chris are alright. They aren't assholes."

"You were spying on me! I knew it! They were friendly to me. They made it fun." Sylvia started walking down the hall to her room but came back. "What about Ryan?"

"What about him?"

"Is he one of the assholes you were worried about?"

Mark focused hard on Sylvia. "Did he do

something?"

"I don't know. He and Beth were gone for a long time."

He was quiet for a moment. "I hear shit about him. Stay away from him."

"Why didn't you say that earlier? You heard us talking on the phone!"

"I didn't hear that it was about Ryan, only the basketball team. You wouldn't have listened. You'd say he was great to piss me off."

"I mean, maybe. But I wasn't gonna do anything with him in the first place. He's Beth's boyfriend now. But Dylan and Chris invited me to their games. I'll be around him more since he's dating Beth."

"Well, be careful. And look after Beth. And you tell me if something happens to you. And don't fucking say I'm not Dad, you don't have to tell me anything. You tell me Sylvia. Got it?"

"Okay. I will."

Amira: Age 21

The pounding at the door startled Amira. No one ever came to her house. She lived on a dirt road in a rural farming community, far enough out that no one stopped by, yet it was a quick fifteen-minute drive from town. It was the perfect combination of privacy without isolation. Except now, it was isolating. The storm raging outside made the night darker. Thunder cracked so loudly she swore the house shook. She could barely hear anything over the weather attacking her home. Tentatively, she opened the door, a locked screen door now the only barrier between her and the stranger. Amira's eyes squinted against the rain that stung her face. The screen was no protection from the elements, nor from the tall man in front of her. She couldn't see much of him through his soaked hoodie pulled up over his head, but those shoulders would be noticeable in whatever he was wearing.

"Hey, I'm sorry to bother you. My car slid into a ditch. I got out to check the damage, and my phone fell out of my pocket and into a puddle. It's not working now. I'm right down the road." He pointed. "I can wait in my car, but I need someone to call a tow for me."

Amira looked him up and down. His dark blue jeans and hoodie were splattered with mud. The trees behind him leaned sideways with the strength of the wind, and the rain was coming down in sheets. She couldn't leave him outside. "Come in," she said before she realized she was saying it. Her body moved out of the way to let him in.

His bright blue eyes widened. His surprise matched Amira's internal shock. She invited a stranger into her house at night during a storm. *This is how women end up dead in movies*she scolded herself silently. His shock didn't stop him from opening the screen door bolting inside, with more thunder and lightning crashing as the weather intensified.

She closed the door behind him. He stood awkwardly in the living room, dripping water and mud on the floor. His cell was still in his hand. "I'm so sorry about this. I'm making a mess."

"It's fine. Hold on a second. I'll grab a towel for you."

"No. I don't want to bother you anymore. I'll go and wait in my car as soon as the tow is called, and I'll end up getting soaked again."

An obnoxious alarm on Amira's phone cut through the air. "Severe thunderstorm and flash flood warning for the next two hours," she read from the notification. "I don't think it's safe for you to wait in your car. This area floods sometimes. I'll get the towels and call the tow. I can put your phone in rice, too. If you want."

The man handed Amira his phone. After putting it in a bowl of rice, she returned with several towels. She called the local towing company and placed it on speakerphone so the man could give his information. They were informed that several calls were ahead of them because of the storm. They had to prioritize the safety of their drivers and would not send anyone out during a flash flood warning. They took down the man's information and Amira's number to update her when they were on their way. Awkward silence followed after she hung up. Amira hurried to break it.

"You can't wait in your car. It's not safe, and you'd have no idea when they would be coming. They are gonna call me. Plus, it could be awhile. I might have some clothes that fit you. And I can wash what you are wearing."

"Are you sure? I don't want to make you uncomfortable or give you more work or anything."

"No. It's okay." She left and came back with a white t-shirt and sweatpants. "These might be too small, but they're dry."

He peeled off his soaked hoodie and shirt. "Where do you want these? I don't want to make a mess."

Amira couldn't answer immediately. The lean muscles on his chest, arms, and shoulders were too distracting. Her eyes followed the trail of water streaming from his hair and running down his body. She glanced back at his face and saw his raised eyebrows and grin. Her face grew hot. "You can drop them on the floor. It's fine."

"I'm Michael, by the way. Is there a bathroom where I can finish changing?"

"I'm Amira. I can step out, and you can change here. Or the bathroom is down the hall," she said, her cheeks warming again.

"I'll stay here. I'll track less mud everywhere." Michael's grin widened, and his eyes sparkled.

She shoved the clothes in his hands, turning to hide her face before heading to her bedroom off the living room. She closed the door behind her and composed herself while she waited. It didn't take long for him to change.

"The shirt is too small. The pants are tight but should work for the next hour or two."

She opened the door and saw the sweatpants fit like a pair of snug capris. Michael held the t-shirt in his hand, looking silly in the ill-fitting clothing. Again, her eyes trailed down his chest and lingered where the pants were too tight. Her eyes went up to his face. He stared back. "My ex might have left shorts. Those might work better." Amira ducked back into her room and started going through a box in the closet.

"These are your ex's clothes?"

"Yeah. He forgot them, and frankly, I don't want

them. So, what brings you to this part of Pennsylvania?" She returned with athletic shorts and focused on his face, not allowing her eyes to travel anywhere else.

Michael told her about his road trip from Indiana to Vermont. He was detouring through to visit his cousin, who lived in a town about twenty minutes away. His aunt and uncle were going to meet him there, and he was going to spend a couple of nights before continuing north. As she handed him the shorts, everything went dark. She swore loudly and jumped, hitting against Michael's warm, solid body. His arms wrapped around her waist to catch her, and without thinking, her hands ran down his chest. She jerked them back and froze in place. Time went by agonizingly slowly, the warmth of his arms still surrounding her. The room became bright again, the silence broken by the sound of appliances clicking back on. Michael's eyes were heavy, and his jaw was tight. The power shut off again. Thunder shook the house, and lightning lit up the room.

Amira's hands reached up to his shoulders and intentionally slid down his chest. He pulled her closer. His hand glided gently up her back, finding her long black hair and running his fingers through it. The lights came back on. She glanced up to find Michael leaning towards her face. She wasn't short, but he still stood almost a foot taller than her. The height difference made it easy for her to avoid his eyes and hide her face.

"I'm... I'm sorry. That was... that wasn't... I don't... I'm sorry." Amira turned away, but he didn't let her go far. She wasn't against his chest, but his arms stayed wrapped around her, not letting her go.

"You don't have to be sorry. You don't have to leave if you don't want to. I mean, it's okay if you want to. But it's also okay if you don't."

His arms relaxed. All she had to do was step

forward, and she could walk away. She stepped back into him instead. He pulled her closer as he held her.

"I don't know what you are comfortable with," he said softly in her ear.

"I don't know either. I don't do this kind of thing. Women end up in bad situations when they do these kinds of things."

He chuckled into her hair. "Then I guess I'll do this for a second. You can ask me to leave at any time. I don't want to pressure you into anything. I will be okay waiting this shit out in my car."

The pull between them was enticing to Amira. It had been almost a year since someone held her. She had broken up with her boyfriend a couple of months ago. However, the relationship had been declining for longer until she couldn't take it anymore. She turned towards Michael, kissing his chest. His white skin paled against her darker complexion. His fingers ran through her hair again, exploring farther down, stopping on her ass. He tilted her chin up, delicately kissing her lips. Amira felt his dick harden. The sensation built up heat between her legs.

Fuck it, she thought. She stood on her tiptoes and gripped his head to move him closer. Her other hand rubbed his erection through the clothing. Her tongue explored his mouth. Michael stripped off her shirt and bra. His dick sprung free as he slid out of the sweatpants, and his breathing increased as she ran her palm steadily up and down it.

She fell to her knees and started licking and sucking. His sharp intake of breath caused her to look up at him. His blue eyes widened with surprise. He swallowed hard. Amira became slick with anticipation. Giving head was usually a chore or a compromise to avoid sex. But this? Initiating, leading, being the driving force? This was exhilarating.

She grabbed his ass and shoved him deeper into

her throat, using her tongue to lick as she sucked. He groaned and cursed simultaneously, pulling his cock out and pushing her onto the floor. He roughly kissed her lips and licked her neck and ear. One hand ripped her pants down as the other slid into her underwear, caressing her. One finger entered, warming her up, then two.

Amira kissed him while trying to kick off her pants, moaning into his mouth. Michael broke away and removed her remaining clothing. His face was immediately buried between her legs. He licked light circles around her clit as his fingers moved in and out of her. Her legs opened wider. She gripped his hair and shoved him closer. Amira's head went back and body arched. Her cries and gasps could be heard over the storm that continued to rage outside. Her pussy clenched his fingers, and wetness dripped down her leg.

"Condoms. I have condoms. In my room."

"Okay. We'll go there."

"No, wait here. I'll be right back."

"You sure?"

Amira didn't answer. She ran to her room, digging through the back of her dresser drawer and hoping the condoms weren't expired. Relief washed over her as she hurried back. Michael was sitting on the floor, eyebrows raised and the grin back on his face. "Lay down," she told him.

"Do you have a pillow?"

She grabbed a decorative pillow from the couch and handed it to him. He tucked it behind his head. Amira crawled in between his legs, licking his shaft up and down as her fingers gripped him. She let out a giggle when he cursed again, then hummed with pleasure as his cock went into her throat. Slipping the condom on, she straddled him. Her hips slid up and down as she adjusted to him being inside her.

Michael gazed up at her, breathing heavy. His hands

went to her thighs, squeezing and rubbing as she grinded against him. Amira grabbed his wrists and moved them to his side. She leaned over him, pinned him down by his shoulders, and rode his dick. Her back arched, and her breasts dangled in his face. Michael kept his arms down. But when she shifted her weight off his shoulder, he took the opportunity to grab her breast and suck her nipple. His other hand squeezed her ass and held her hips down. He thrust upward to match her energy.

"Oh God! Yes! More! Harder! Fuck me back!" Amira gasped. *Where the hell did that come from?*She glanced at Michael, anxious how he would respond.

He grabbed her head and kissed her. His tongue probed her mouth, and his teeth nipped her lip. He shifted his attention back to her breasts, locking eyes with her as he sucked and bit harder. She fell back into the moment, her embarrassment at crying out gone. She let out another moan, grinding harder against him. The power clicked off again. Both of Michael's hands gripped her ass and locked her in place.

Despite the storm, she heard Michael command, "Ride me, Amira. Fuck me."

Amira's wetness made gliding on his cock easy. Every time she thrust down, his dick pounded up, penetrating deeper. His fingers played with her clit, and her pace quickened. The darkness lessened her inhibitions, and her release was loud. She collapsed against him. The intensity of her orgasm rendered her weak and her body sated.

"It's my turn now. Roll over."

Michael turned her over onto her back and placed the pillow under her head. He eased himself in between her legs, slowly sliding inside her. He kissed her breasts, allowing her to catch her breath. She planted her feet flat on the floor and spread her knees wider to allow him deeper access. When she regained control over her body, she started fucking him back. His speed and power increased. He threw one leg over his shoulder, tilting her to the side. One arm gripped her hips as his other hand played with her clit.

"You think you can come again?"

"I don't think so. No... probably not."

"I think you can come again. Tell me what you want." The lights kicked back on. Michael's eyes were piercing, and his thin frame taunt. He licked his fingers, spat on them, and rubbed her clit. He leaned down, his tongue entering her mouth as his thumb continued to stimulate her. Amira wrapped her arms around him and brought her leg close, trapping him against her body. Michael broke the kiss and stared directly into her dark brown eyes. "Tell me what you want. I live in Indiana. Maybe I'll end up living in Vermont. You will never see me again, Amira. You can ask for anything right now. I'd give it to you."

"This is a lot. I don't do this. This is enough."

"No, ask for what you want."

Amira took a slow breath in and out. "Stay like this. Stay close to me like this and kiss me." She shifted both of her legs and intertwined them behind his back. He bit her lip and sucked her tongue before kissing her. His kisses moved down her neck and chest. His focus again turned to her nipples. The length of his shaft moved in and out of her, firm, steady, and deep. "Bite harder. Leave a mark. I want to remember you were here."

Michael groaned as he obliged. His thumb still teased her, using more pressure and speed. He broke away from her breast and whispered in her ear. "Be loud again. I like to hear you. Scream my name, Amira. Scream my name so you remember me."

He moved back to her nipple, biting it. His thrusts became urgent and less controlled. His arm wrapped around her and gripped her ass. His hands dug into her flesh as he penetrated deeper. The pleasure from the pain of his teeth and fingers brought her to climax again. She cried Michael's name as another powerful orgasm crashed over her, leaving her limp in its wake. He shifted to kneel between her thighs. He spread them farther apart, repeatedly burying himself inside her. Suddenly his dick was against her stomach and his body was convulsing. Amira's arms and legs entwined around him and pulled him close as he came. They lay like this until both of their breathing eased closer to normal. Michael grinned at her. She smiled back.

"I hate to ask, but I am so thirsty. Do you have anything to drink?"

Amira laughed, "Yeah. Are you hungry? I am. I think your clothes are still on the floor, too. I can wash them. It's still pouring outside. I don't think your tow is coming soon." She paused. "If you want to, you can shower. I mean, you will smell like flowers because all I have is floral body wash. You can use the shower while I start laundry."

"Or you can wash them and then join me in the shower?" Michael's eyes sparkled and eyebrows arched up. "Bathroom is down the hall, right?"

"I can join you. Yeah," she eagerly replied.

Michael headed towards the bathroom as Amira got dressed and gathered his clothes. After dropping them into her washer, she grabbed a mop to clean up the mud and water.

"Are you one of those girls that likes the water scalding hot?"

She laughed. "Yeah, I'm one of them. But it doesn't have to be like that if you can't handle it."

"You may have to settle for warm then. You aren't supposed to shower during a storm, anyway. We should keep it short. Hell, I wouldn't worry about it if I weren't muddy."

"I'm not muddy."

"I noticed some on you. I hope there isn't any on

your pillows."

"I'll check when we are out. Oh my God! This isn't warm! This is cool!" Amira moved to the far end of the tub, letting him stand under the water.

He started laughing. "I'll be quick, then turn the heat up for you."

"When you are done, give me the washcloth. There's mud all over your back."

Michael handed it to her. "Can you reach? Do I need to go on my knees?" he said over his shoulder.

She laughed. "No. I can reach fine. See? All done. But I should have had you kneel just because."

He increased the temperature. "Switch with me. I'll scrub your back. Are you gonna wash your hair?"

"No, I'm not trying to stay in here long." He nodded in agreement.

Climbing out, he slid into the athletic shorts. They were still too small but fit better than the sweatpants. Amira wrapped her towel around her and headed to her room. "The 1970s called. They want their shorts back." She smirked.

"Date taller men!"

"You can head towards the kitchen. It's in the direction I walked with your laundry. We can keep an eye on your clothes, and I can make us something to eat." She returned from her room to find Michael sitting at the table, attempting to turn on his phone.

"I think it needs more time in the rice."

"I think I need a new phone," he said sadly.

"That will be terrible if you do. You are in the middle of a road trip." Amira started pulling things out of her fridge. "I don't want to cook anything in case the electricity goes off again. I can make us turkey sandwiches. I have water, juice, and diet soda. I have pretzels and crackers. What would you like?"

"Diet soda, huh? No thanks, but I am starving. I

haven't eaten for a couple of hours. I planned on eating at my cousin's house. I'll take whatever juice you have and everything you offered. What kind is it?"

"Mango Guava."

Michael started laughing again. "I changed my mind. Water please."

"Is your family going to be worried?"

"Yeah. My cousin will probably try to call me. He stays up late, so he should still be up when I get there. Or I'll pound on the door until he wakes up."

Amira made them each a sandwich and set pretzels on plates, then brought a candle in from the living room to the dining room table. "Just in case." she said.

As they ate, she asked him about his trip and why he was considering Vermont. Michael asked how she had ended up in this area. Conversation flowed with discussions of employment, figuring out life in their early twenties, family, random side stories, and crazy extreme weather videos they had seen on the internet. Michael's clothes were placed in the dryer. The storm gradually subsided throughout their meal. Michael asked Amira for an update on the flash flood. She checked her phone and realized the warning had passed thirty minutes ago. "There were people waiting before you. We can have dessert. I can make sundaes. You still might have to be here a while."

"Sundaes?"

"I keep ice cream, whipped cream, sprinkles, chocolate syrup, and maraschino cherries in the fridge. Always."

"We could have a lot of fun with that," he said.

"Is that a yes?"

"I would love a sundae. Thank you."

Amira's cell rang in the middle of scooping ice cream into bowls. The towing company informed them that the estimated arrival time would be in about an hour. She explained the situation and arranged for them to notify her when the driver was thirty minutes away. "How long did it take you to walk here?"

"Not long. Fifteen minutes? I'd want to be at my car before them. I'll leave after they call again. I guess we can't have fun with your sundae stuff. I don't want to hold them up. I bet they are fucking busy after this storm."

"That would have been a lot of fun." Amira brought the sundaes over. Silence fell over them.

"I don't know how to say this, so I'm just going to say it. Things are too uncertain in my life right now."

"What does that mean?"

"It means I don't want to start anything."

"Anything like what? Are you talking about a long-distance relationship?"

"I don't want any relationships."

"That's fine with me because I don't want a long-distance one."

A smile crossed Michael's face before his eyes lowered to his ice cream bowl. He took a slow, deep breath in. "I don't want to give you my number. It will be too tempting."

"Oh." Amira's face fell. "Nothing? Not even a text to make sure you got to your cousin's okay?"

"Nothing. Shit. I sound like a fucking asshole, don't I?"

"Yeah. I liked talking to you."

"I liked talking to you, too. That's part of the problem. I'd want to see you again if I had your number, but I can't start something like this now."

"I mean, I wasn't expecting a relationship. I wasn't expecting anything. I was just kinda hoping we could stay in touch. I don't want to have to travel to Vermont or Indiana or wherever you end up. I can't honestly. I don't have the money, and I can't take the time off. I hoped to text, maybe call? But I understand. It's okay." The dryer buzzed that it was finished. "Oh! Just in time. You can put on warm clothes." Amira got up to gather his belongings and handed them to him. Michael turned to head towards the bathroom.

"Wait. Change here."

"Huh?"

"You said I could ask for anything, and you'd give it to me. I understand your number isn't part of the offer." She squared her shoulders. "I want to see you naked one more time. And a picture. Of you. Of the two of us."

He smiled. "I can do that." He pulled down the shorts he borrowed and put on his jeans, shirt, and hoodie. He grabbed his cell and dropped it into his pants pocket. Amira snapped a picture. "Come here. Let me take it. My arms are longer." She leaned back against his chest, and Michael wrapped his arm around her, extending the other out for the selfie. "How did it turn out? Do you like it?"

She inspected it. "Yes. Too bad your phone doesn't work. You could take one of your own. Something to remember me by."

He laughed. "I'm not forgetting you, Amira. I got stranded in the middle of a severe thunderstorm and flash flood warning on a long road trip. You helped me out, and we had an incredible time together. You are completely unforgettable." Michael's arm encircled her waist and squeezed her ass. His fingers ran through her hair as he kissed her. She rose up on her toes and wrapped her arms around his shoulders. The kiss kept going, slow and leisurely, their tongues exploring and their hands attempting to memorize sensations. The mood was shattered by her ringtone. She answered it and confirmed that the tow truck was thirty minutes away.

"I'll walk you to the door if you don't mind."

"Sure." He smiled and slipped his hand into hers.

When they got to the door, he pulled her in for

another kiss. "Oh shit! Hold on a second!" Amira yelled and dashed back into the laundry room. She returned with a pink umbrella with red polka dots. "Something to remember me by." She grinned.

Michael laughed, pulling her in and kissing her. "I will cherish it forever." He kissed her cheek, shifted to her ear then neck, coming back to her lips one last time. "Thank you for everything Amira."

"Have a safe trip. If something doesn't work out with the tow, come back. Okay?"

"I will. Seriously." He smiled, closing the door behind him.

She walked back to the kitchen. The windows gave her a brief view of the pink and red polka dot umbrella moving away before vanishing in the darkness. She glanced at the table and the dishes that needed to be washed. Across the chair were the athletic shorts Michael had worn. Amira picked them up and returned them to her room, vowing to never throw them away.

Annie: Age 25

How she'd failed so spectacularly was beyond her. Annie had lost everything. She'd silently handed over the keys to her car when it was repossessed, unable to meet the repo man's eyes. She avoided the calls from her mortgage and credit card companies. Her phone was on the verge of getting shut off, and her bank account was in the negative. She believed that buying a house would make her future better. She believed that paying a mortgage instead of rent was an investment and a way to create stability, even wealth.

Then, the market collapsed. The roof started leaking. The price of supplies skyrocketed. In fact, the cost of everything skyrocketed. The house used oil heating, and winter in Upstate New York was hard. She had already left her job to pursue her property management start-up. Now the economy was collapsing around her, taking her new business down with it. She called a bankruptcy lawyer for a consultation. Next, she called her mom to borrow money to pay the bankruptcy lawyer. Everything had to go.

She applied to nursing school and, to her surprise, was accepted. With no family living close by and no money, she took out extra student loans to help cover rent until she graduated. Her friend told her about an easy job at the local bus station where she could do her homework and receive discounted tickets. However, the owner paid less than minimum wage off the books and provided no benefits. Annie lived nearby, so she applied anyway. He hired her on the spot, and she started immediately. She walked to work and caught the bus to school, which made it worthwhile. She was able to complete her school assignments most days because it was slow. The side benefits were worth the lack of compensation.

Funds were tight. Stethoscopes and textbooks were expensive. Utilities in her apartment weren't included, and the random roommate she lived with paid his portion of the bills late. She was on campus more than she was at her house, which led to eating out or in the cafeteria. The college was designed to be for commuters and did not include dorm housing or a meal plan. There wasn't much of money left once tuition, school supplies, and her rent were taken care of.

It didn't take long to make friends with some of the bus drivers. Discounted tickets turned into free rides, and the drivers started to drop off things to help her out. One gave her kitchen appliances he didn't use anymore. Another brought her lunch when he knew she was working. There was a woman driver who always bought in bulk. She brought her household items like cleaning supplies, toilet paper, napkins, paper plates, and whatever other item was on sale.

One day, a driver brought her a small crate of apples. His son-in-law owned an orchard, and his daughter had given him some of their harvest. Annie was delighted. She had expected beat-up and bruised fruit that wouldn't sell well. Instead, these were huge and in great shape. It was with some difficulty that she carried the crate back to her apartment.

The first thing she made was applesauce since it was easy and quick. Next, she baked a pie like she did with her mom when she was a child. Still, so many were left. She began cutting up an apple for lunch. At first, she bought a packet of peanut butter to eat it with, until the honey next to the sugar and creamer in the school cafeteria caught her attention. For a month, every day, she decorated her sliced apple with honey.

Annie savored the gift. She vividly recalled the scents and colors of the blossoms on her favorite childhood tree and the deer that would munch on the apples every autumn. Never did she imagine that something that used to grow outside her door would be a treat. Never did she imagine being so poor that an apple would be considered a meal.

Beth and Sylvia: Ages 28 and 27

Beth pulled up to Sylvia's apartment building, texted her that she was outside, then climbed the three flights of stairs. She didn't bother to knock when she reached her door. She let herself in, kicked off her wedge sneakers, and flopped down on the couch, tucking her long, slim legs under her.

"Well, shit, girl! You didn't tell me it was that kinda day." Sylvia said, emerging from her bedroom at the back of the apartment. She wore black yoga pants and a black t-shirt that displayed half of the tattoo on her lean arms. Her hair was tied up in a messy top bun, accentuating the red ends. She detoured to the kitchen, grabbed two wine glasses, a bottle of Moscato, cheese, crackers, grapes, and apples. "You should be grateful. I had already planned on using my only two fancy glasses with you. You hungry? Did you eat today?" Without waiting for an answer, Sylvia started cutting apples and slicing cheese.

"No. I ran out of the house too fast. I had to leave while the kids were distracted by Doc McStuffins. I did drink coffee this morning. Does that count?"

"Sure. That counts. Where are you going after me?"

"Home. I can't leave Brett with the kids for much more than an hour or two. He'll start calling and texting me."

"Did you dress up for me?"

"I didn't dress up."

"Seriously Beth? Did you look in the mirror before you left? Your hair has amazing waves. You must have gone to the salon not long ago. I don't remember those highlights looking so fresh like that. You wore a skirt and put on makeup, and that's not dressing up? And how do you wear pink so well? I can't wear pink. Have you seen me in pink? It washes out the little color I have. Instantly pale. Paler. More pale? Whatever. You understand."

"I like pink. You should try adding color to your wardrobe, Sylvie. There's an entire rainbow you can use as an accent against black," she playfully retorted.

Sylvie stopped cutting an apple and stuck her tongue out at her. "That's what the red in my hair is for."

"I needed to fix my hair, and last weekend I got to go to the salon. It's been crazy, and I haven't gotten it done in about eight months. I like my hair maintained. I like wearing nice clothes. It makes me feel like a human, a woman. If I wore heels for you, it would be dressing up. I almost did, but Brett wouldn't have believed me when I said I was going to hang out with you." She paused and asked herself if she was ready to talk about this. Sylvia was still in the kitchen, adding grapes and crackers to a large plate. Beth took a deep breath in and exhaled. "It would have caused another fight," she said softly.

"Another, huh?"

"Yes. I cheated on him. About a year ago. Maybe a year and a half."

"That explains a lot."

"What do you mean?"

"I could tell something was going on. I was waiting for you to tell me." Sylvia came over to the couch and set the food on the coffee table. She went back to grab the alcohol and glasses. "The only nice thing about a small apartment is that the kitchen is close. And it's easier to clean. I swear though, one day I will not live in a box. I splurged on this, by the way. This is a $25 bottle of wine I got for us today. I buy the $10 stuff for myself. I'm not saying I'm trying to get you drunk, but if I bought the good wine, I expect a good story." She plopped down on the floor across from Beth, with the coffee table in between them. Beth glanced up to find her peering over the top of her glass.

"It was my coworker's brother."

"How the hell does that happen? I've never met any of my coworkers' families."

"A bunch of us went out for trivia night at a bar. A couple of coworkers I like were going and wanted me to come. I needed to get out of the house. Will was almost one. Abby was three. I really wanted a break. I really wanted to do something different. My coworker planned on drinking, so she brought her brother to be the DD. We just hit it off. But she got so drunk it took two of us to get her home. Then she started throwing up. God, Sylvie, at that point I might as well have stayed with the kids. I texted Brett what was going on and spent the night." Beth took slow sips of her wine, staring down at the food on the table.

"And then you fucked her brother?" Sylvia bluntly asked.

"No, nothing happened. We picked out a movie together and stayed up talking. We had a lot in common. He fell asleep in a chair, and I slept on the couch." She paused again, the silence drawing out. Sylvia gave her a minute, then broke the stillness again.

"So, it was emotional cheating?"

"No. Well, not at that point. He found me on Facebook and messaged me. We started messaging casually. Then switched numbers to text and talk."

"He knew you were married and had kids then?"

"Yeah, he knew."

"Is he married? Does he have children?"

"He has a girlfriend. They had been together about three years."

"What did you guys talk about?"

"At first, we talked about our day and things we both liked. It was just a friendship to start."

"When did it turn?"

"There was a margarita night at a restaurant my coworkers and I like. I told my coworker I wanted to get drunk this time and not babysit her. I asked if her brother would be the DD again because Brett would have to take care of the children. She said she planned to drink too and was going to ask him to drive, anyway. I knew she was going to get shitfaced. I was counting on it, and she did. Her brother liked me. It was obvious from his messages. We sat next to each other and found ways to touch so no one would notice. I had a little too much alcohol. I wasn't drunk, but I drank enough so that I wouldn't think. We had been talking and messaging for two months. I planned on having sex with him when I went out. We helped my coworker home. I messaged Brett to tell him that she got drunk, again, and I was spending the night. When she passed out in her bed, her brother and I had sex on the couch. After that, we started sexting, sending pictures, and finding ways to meet up. I was careful, Sylvie. I deleted everything. His contact information was under a woman's name, and I pretended it was a coworker if he texted when Brett was around."

"So how did he find out?"

"Will had been sick. He was up all night with a fever and diarrhea and didn't fall asleep until three in the morning. I kept waking up to check his temperature and make sure he wasn't sleeping in poop. We were both exhausted. When Will took a nap in the afternoon, I passed out, too. He texted me. Brett saw the name, thought it was a colleague, and checked my phone. That's when he realized."

"Oh shit. How bad was the message?"

"Not terrible, thank God. We had sent each other a lot of dirty messages. Very detailed. But this text was obviously not one a woman would send to her coworker."

"How long had you two been fucking?"

"Eight months."

"You kept that up for eight months? Deleting everything? And end up getting caught cause you were up all night taking care of Will? That's some shit right there." Sylvia took another sip of Moscato, "How long has Brett known?"

"Four or five months. I'm sorry I didn't tell you sooner. I didn't want you to judge me," Beth said tearfully. She refilled her glass, drank half, and refilled it again. She wiped away the tears that slid down her face, took a breath in, and sipped the wine some more. Beth promptly regained her composure. The need to be put together had been programmed into her since she was a child. Her mom insisted she always looked proper in public. She would dress her in dresses, cute little shoes, and braid her hair. Her dad made sure she was well-behaved. If she did anything other than sit silently, there would be consequences. He never hit her, but his words and the tone he used still echoed in her head. It had gotten worse as she grew up. Her mom made remarks about her weight and the expectations of being homecoming queen, prom queen, and maintaining high honor roll. In college, her mom's comments shifted to attracting a husband.

Now, as a mother, there was constant pressure to remain calm and poised through temper tantrums and public crying. At work, she was hoping to move into management. Every day she would wake up early and spend at least an hour dressing business casual and maintaining an even, professional demeanor. She used to wonder if she liked to dress nicely or if it was years of conditioning. It took being a new mother, stuck in yoga pants and leggings at home with leaky breasts and shirts stained with baby vomit, to realize looking put together was something she enjoyed. It made her feel like a person. She felt safe. Clothes were her armor against the world, a shield to hide behind. People could judge her by her appearance, but they would be judging her armor. Sylvie knew her. She knew the girl underneath the poise. She knew her outside of being the social butterfly or the professional woman or mom. Sylvie's judgment would hurt.

Something squishy and cold hit Beth's forehead. She looked down and spotted a grape on the floor.

"Why the fuck do you think I'm gonna judge you? Like I can talk with the shit I do. Crazy woman." Sylvia huffed as she popped a piece of apple in her mouth and threw another grape, hitting Beth on the shoulder. Beth smiled, picked it up and threw it back.

"You don't think I'm a terrible human being for lying and cheating on my husband?"

"I mean, don't get me wrong. It sucks to be the one cheated on. It hurts like hell. My dad cheated on my mom. That's why they divorced. Then I've been cheated on, and it's made me completely reanalyze the entire relationship. I questioned everything that happened after I found out. How was I supposed to trust the guy again when he had lied to me about so many things? Shit, I doubted my worth as a person. Was I not good enough? Why wasn't I good enough? It fucking sucked. I thought less about myself and hated how some guy's opinion of me affected me so much. It was difficult to come back from. I mean, I didn't end up coming back from it. Every time a guy cheated on me, I never recovered. We always broke up. I never wanted to make it work."

"Thanks, Sylvie. I feel better." Beth's voice was flat and her tone dry.

Sylvia threw another grape, but this time Beth dodged it. "The point is, it's going to be hard. Should you have done it? No. Should you have lied to him? No, but I also know everything you do for the relationship and all the responsibility you carry. I know all the things you've asked him to do multiple times that he still doesn't do. Shit is complicated. Being a mother to two kids and a man-child isn't fucking easy. I don't need to make it worse by giving you a guilt trip."

"This isn't a guilt trip? Because it sounds like it is."

"No, it's real." She took a bite of cheese and cracker. "Give me a second. I'm hungry." Her voice was muffled. "It's lunchtime. I'm not going to talk about important shit with food in my mouth. You haven't eaten anything yet either. I'm watching you. Eat some fucking food, Beth. It's one pm and you've had nothing but coffee and wine."

Sylvia sipped her drink and stared. Beth reluctantly started to nibble a piece of apple to appease her. Sylvia didn't stop eyeing her, so she made a show of putting cheese on crackers. When the apple hit her empty stomach, she realized how hungry she was and shoved an entire cracker with cheese into her mouth.

Sylvia got up and came back with four pills. "You get headaches when you don't eat for a long time. The wine may make it worse. Take the Ibuprofen." Beth listened, using the alcohol to wash it down. "Dating two guys changed how I view things. Now there are three, and I am learning new shit." Sylvia said.

"There's a third guy now?"

"Yeah. I started seeing him a couple of months ago. I think he might end up being sporadic."

"What do the other two think about the third? Oh my God! Your brother! What does he think about all of this?"

She laughed. "Mark is surprisingly very supportive about it. It shocked the shit out of me. I thought he would go classic 1990s dad, flip out and threaten to use a shotgun on all of them. Mom is supportive, too. She wants to make sure they are all treating me well. I was afraid they would accuse me of being like my father. But they didn't."

"You still haven't heard from him, have you?"

"No. He came around once in a while for about a year after the divorce was final. Then he moved. We got phone calls for a few months. It's been nothing for years." Sylvia sipped her wine. "Brandon doesn't care. He's fine with fun and casual. Darius is having a hard time."

"Darius wants you to be his girlfriend?"

"I pretty much am his girlfriend. I think he's threatened by the new guy. I also think he doesn't understand why I found a third partner." Sylvia was matter of fact as she spoke. "It's still new, and we are figuring it out. It's a lot of difficult conversations. There's a lot of his asking why and my trying to explain the things I want and need. He needs so much reassurance. All three of them have to be honest with me. If they lie and say they are fine with something, it's going to blow up in my face. If they lie and cheat on me, well, first off, that's just fucking stupid. I'm in open relationships with all of them. They can find another girl. There's no reason to lie about it. But if they did and I can't trust them, it will blow up in our faces. I understand how Brett feels. Having your trust destroyed hurts like fucking hell. But I also understand there are things you want and need, and he isn't giving them to you. And that's a slow death. You've asked for them, and he still doesn't give them to you. That fucking sucks. You've only been married for five years. Do you want a divorce?"

"No, he will have to divorce me. I'm not initiating a divorce."

"Okay. I'm guessing you can't open up your marriage? Right after you cheated is a terrible time, but is that even an option?"

"No, he would never go for that."

"If one man isn't willing to do something, I can go to another. Or find an alternative way in general to meet my needs and wants. I care about each guy differently, and they contribute differently to my life. I have a different kind of love for each of them, and it fills different needs. You have that option too, without having an affair. It will be harder, like expanding your friends. I mean, you won't find what you are looking for with your family. And you probably won't have your sexual needs and wants met without cheating. I understand why you wanted to go elsewhere, but you did it in a shitty way with a lot of nasty consequences."

"Brett says I could have used the same attention I gave the other man to make things more exciting with him."

"Here's a random thought. If he contributed more to taking care of the house and the children, maybe you would have more energy to be exciting."

"Sylvie, he's watching them now so I can come here."

"And the last time he watched his own children so you could do something was when?"

Beth paused. "About five months ago."

"Who took care of them when you got your hair done?"

"My mom came over. She had been hinting very pointedly that I needed to fix my hair every time she saw me. She said I was embarrassing to be around, and she gladly came over so I could go to the salon."

"Beth, Brett doesn't deserve a gold star because he's being a parent. When was the last time you stayed with the kids so he could go out?"

"Yesterday. But it was a trade so I could come here today."

"And before that?"

"Last weekend."

"See? Motherfucker doesn't earn a gold star because you stayed with the kids yesterday in order to get *permission* to visit me today." Sylvie said sharply.

"I told him I wanted more time to do other things besides work and take care of the children. He said he did take care of the kids, and I fucked another man. He thinks we weren't having sex as much because I was having the affair. He's not listening to me when I tell him why I don't want to have sex with him as much."

"First off, that's real shitty of him to throw it in your face. Yeah, I bet he's hurt that he watched Abby and Will while you met up with the other guy. But they are still his children, and he should be taking care of them, regardless. You call off work when they are sick. You call off to take them to their appointments. You take them out on the weekends. He doesn't do any of those things. You watch them while he watches sports. You watch them when he's late coming home from his job. He doesn't need to make you feel shitty for wanting a life."

"I only asked him a few times to stay with the kids when I met up with the other man."

"Huh?"

"He watched them on trivia night. That was my first time out. I didn't anticipate anything besides hanging out with coworkers. I didn't cheat that night. He watched them on margarita night, when I was intending to cheat. I think I asked Brett two more times over the next eight months to stay with the children when I was planning on having sex with my other guy. We found other ways. My mom likes to take the children out sometimes and act like she's an adoring grandmother. That gave me a few hours to be with him, if he was free. Mostly I would take them to daycare or arrange for the babysitter to stay with them."

"He's making it seem like he watched them all the time and every time he did, you had sex with the other man?"

"Yes, oh my God, Sylvie. He was amazing in bed," Beth said, "I didn't tell Brett that, of course."

"Of course."

"He didn't look at me weird when I asked him to do things. I didn't ask him to do anything crazy. But if I ask

Brett to go down on me, he makes this face or this sighing sound. He's down there for a couple of minutes. I'm just starting to relax when he stops and shoves his dick inside me. The other man loved to eat me out. I'd have two orgasms before we even had sex. The other guy wanted anal, and we were working towards that. I was so surprised that I kind of liked it. I didn't think I would. I mentioned to Brett about using his finger or a plug. He made a face." Beth paused, "Sylvie, do you remember the time we were seven, and we played in the park after the rain? I had on the yellow dress with the little hearts on it?"

"Yes! I was covered in mud!" Sylvia laughed. "I had to go into the creek because the water was higher than usual. You stayed on the bank, but your shoes were sinking into the mud. You took off your shoes and socks to keep them clean. Your legs and the bottom of your dress got filthy."

"Yes. When I got home, the look I got from my mom was terrible. She was disgusted that I was out in public with mud on my legs and clothes. She forced me into the shower and rubbed my skin raw."

"Oh, shit."

"He looked at me, and it reminded me of that. It was awful. I've tried to tell him ideas to spice up our sex life. I asked him to read one of my romance novels. I told him it would help explain what I wanted and some things I'd like to try."

"I bet that went over well."

"He made a huge deal about men reading romance novels, but I kept asking and he finally did agree."

"Did he?"

"No."

"He is busy. Did he have time to read it?"

"I asked him three months ago. The book is two hundred and fifty pages long. He only needed to read one chapter, and I told him that, too."

"Never mind. He's not going to."

"No."

Silence fell over them. Sylvia poured herself another glass, then topped off Beth's. Beth picked up more food from the half-eaten plate. Her stomach was almost full. The wine was buzzing through her body, releasing the tension it held. How did talking about such a stressful subject help her calm down? Her marriage was a mess. Her home life was a wreck. However, right now with her best friend and the makeshift charcuterie board, it was a little less terrible. Sylvia gazed out of the window. Beth could tell she was processing something and waited.

Sylvia whipped her head around, a deep seriousness burning in her green eyes. "Listen. You need to do two things for me. Got it?" She said fiercely, leaning towards Beth. "I need you to open a bank account in your own name. Only your name should be on it. I need you to open a credit card in only your name as well."

"Sylvie, what are you talking about?"

"You don't want to divorce Brett, but that doesn't mean Brett won't divorce you. You need your own account with your own money in case he leaves you and cuts you off. And you need your own credit card to charge things until you can stand on your own."

"Sylvie..."

"You've gotta trust me on this." Sylvia's intensity didn't wane. "Do you remember what it was like for me and Mark and my mom? She had nothing. My father cheated on her, and he still ended up with everything. You have to have your own. I can't imagine your parents would help you if Brett divorces you."

"They most likely wouldn't help. But if we divorced because I cheated on him, there would be no chance."

"See? Get your own shit, Beth."

"Is this why you have three men, Sylvie?" she said half-jokingly. "Because you have a hard time depending on one person to come through for you? You don't trust a man to be honest? They can't cheat on you if it's an open relationship?"

"First, we aren't psychoanalyzing me right now. We can do that next time we drink and eat cheap charcuterie. We are psychoanalyzing you." Sylvia leaned back, the fire in her replaced with her standard level of bluntness. "You are used to keeping up appearances. You are accustomed to being provided for. You don't know if Brett will do either. Start something for yourself, quietly and discreetly. The best-case scenario is I'm wrong, you don't need it, and you can use the money to go on a fancy family vacation. Or give it to the kids when they are older. Or use it to go on a vacation by yourself. You can do whatever you want with it if you don't use it. The point is, you will have it. The worst-case scenario is you don't listen to me, you need the money, and Brett and your parents won't help you. Open the accounts, Beth."

Beth looked down at her feet and put her head against her hand. "Okay." Her body sank into the couch. Sylvie moved next to her and hugged her. Beth leaned into her shoulder. "I fucked up, Sylvie."

"Yep. You had the audacity to want something more for yourself than work and motherhood. And you picked a guy that doesn't show any interest in supporting you."

"I was talking about cheating on my husband. I could lose everything."

"I mean, that too."

Beth smiled. "You are a terrible influence on me."

"Don't tell Brett. Tell him I cursed you out for cheating on a wonderful husband. That way you can come back and we can psychoanalyze me and my three relationships. You should leave out that I'm having sex with three men."

She laughed. "That would be smart." She took a big breath in. "I should head back. I've been here about an hour already. It's a thirty minute drive one way and I don't want him thinking I'm lying. I gave him access to my cell. He can check it whenever he wants. He wanted that so he could read my messages and monitor who calls. It doesn't help him trust me. I had the other man's number under a woman's name. Even when I tell him the truth and he checks my phone, he still doesn't believe me. I can tell."

"Touch up your makeup Beth. We'll take a picture together. I can come over more if you need me to. I can play cool auntie with Abby and Will. It's my reminder why I will never have children of my own. Just tell me what you need."

"I love you, Sylvie."

"Love you, too Beth."

Beth didn't turn on music on the drive home. She turned over the conversation in her head. Sylvie was right. Brett could divorce her. She had given him a valid reason, and if he did what would happen to her and her children? Beth thought back on their relationship, on the five years they'd been married and the three they dated. She was hit with the painful realization that she had settled. He wasn't a bad guy, but he hadn't been the best choice either. She had gone along with what was familiar. He would provide and he wasn't bad. That was enough reason to marry him. She'd needed to find a stable man to marry and so she had. Now here she was with two children, a house, and all the issues that came with marriage and a family. He made more money than her. They had joint debt. She liked her in-laws more than her own parents and wished they lived closer. She had a better relationship with his sister than he did. She would be sad if she couldn't see them. Divorce was not an option. She loved her children and wouldn't give them up for anything.

Why must she want something that felt good? Why couldn't she be more like her mother and be content with stability, money, a house, and a happy-looking family? She made a silent promise to herself. If Brett wasn't willing to give her the things she wanted, she would learn to go without. Once the children were older, maybe then she could pursue some of her personal goals. Until then, it would be her husband, a couple girl friends, or nothing.

Amira: Age 30

Amira took the alone time in the elevator to take deep, calming breaths in. *I've been practicing this. I've been practicing this.* She had been preparing for this meeting with her boss for several weeks. It wasn't formal, and there was no reason to schedule an appointment. Her boss was always in his office on Monday mornings and had a couple of minutes for anyone to stop by. She had gathered information about how her contributions impacted the company and how her suggestions had increased customer satisfaction over the last year.

No, not suggestions. My ideas. She hadn't made suggestions. She'd presented fully formed ideas and a starting implementation plan for how to improve customer relations. Then, she'd led a team and executed it. She'd streamlined current processes and made them more efficient and user-friendly.

Her palms were sweaty, and her heart thumped in her chest. She opened her tote purse and saw the folder inside. She had typed all her contributions to the company on a sheet of paper and placed it in a folder to bring with her. She didn't want it on her cell. She didn't think it would be professional for her phone to be out while talking to her boss. She also thought he would appreciate a presentation of her contributions in a hard-copy form. He was an older man who was nostalgic about the past. He might hold the traditional aspects of paper in higher regard. The sight of the folder lowered her heart rate. She could refer to it if she got nervous. At the bottom of her tote was her small pink umbrella with red polka dots. She took another deep breath. *Ask for what I want. Ask for what I want.*

It had been challenging to find a smaller version of the umbrella she had given Michael all those years ago. She had to order it online, and finding one that could fit in her tote purse had taken time. There were practical purposes, too. Several times she left work when it was raining, but she never got stuck running to her car like her coworkers did. She simply opened it up, and a warm, fuzzy feeling washed over her instead of rain. It came from being prepared, but also from remembering him.

It didn't matter that she'd never heard from him again. His memory made her happy. She occasionally thought about trying to find him. However, searching "Michael" in Indiana or Vermont, or anywhere, didn't seem practical. Other times, like now, the umbrella was a reminder. Things didn't always work out, but she learned to ask for what she wanted. She learned she might get it. If she didn't, she had the choice of staying or leaving. It was not easy. It took her a few years, and a couple failed relationships to learn the lesson. It got easier with time, but she still had to build herself up for it. Today wasn't about a person. It was about a place.

She'd rehearsed this speech multiple times in the shower. Then, she'd rehearsed multiple times in the mirror. Eventually, she moved past how ridiculous it felt to practice, called her best friend, and recited it to her. The folder also held a job offer from another company. Amira had options. She had been applying to other jobs with higher salaries and going on interviews but wasn't ready to resign yet. She liked her colleagues but knew from talking to them that she was not getting paid the same amount. Most of her male coworkers were making several thousand more a year than she was. One recently hired woman also made more than her. Amira had been working here for two and a half years. The time had come to make a decision. Ask for the raise she wanted and thought she earned or move to a place that would give her the salary she was qualified for.

The elevator doors opened, and Amira's heels clicked down the hall. She straightened her back, reminded herself for the millionth time that she had practiced this, and walked into her boss's office. She was greeted by the secretary at the desk, asked to take a seat and told Mr. McAlister would be free shortly. *Ask for what I want. Ask for what I want.*

As far as bosses went, Mr. McAlister wasn't terrible. He had no issues with occasional lateness or absenteeism. He understood life happened. Employees didn't need an appointment to see him. He followed through on most of what he said he would, but not enough to confidently trust his word. He was professional and respectful and engaged in friendly, casual conversations with staff. He did not remember specific information about anyone unless an employee was either a favorite or problematic. His professionalism could also be wielded skillfully to dodge difficult questions and avoid accountability. He was the type of boss who would respond to a question without actually answering it and should have gotten involved in local politics. Amira knew she had to be careful. His amicable demeanor and ability to talk around a topic could easily have her leaving his office with no definitive answer.

She was called in after a brief wait. Mr. McAlister greeted her with an oversized smile. His shiny forehead gleamed in the fluorescent lighting, exacerbating his receding hairline and white hair. He extended his pudgy hand to offer one of the candies at his desk. She politely declined but took the moment to pull out her folder and open it in her lap. After a couple of minutes of casual discussion, he asked for an update on one of the processes she was working on. Amira took the opportunity to lead into the reason for her meeting.

"It's actually my process improvement initiatives that bring me in today, Mr. McAlister. This is the third project I've started this year. I've brought in several ideas, and I appreciate you providing me with a team to implement them. We have been working well together. Customer retention has increased steadily. We were at 43.8% and are currently on track to be at 58.6% at the end of the year. The 14.8% increase has been very profitable for the company."

"The customer acquisition cost is being used to add new clientele rather than replace lost clients." Amira continued. "We are receiving more positive reviews online, and survey results show this is bringing additional prospects to us. I have also simplified the way we acquire new customers. It is more efficient and user-friendly to the staff. I am confident that these trends will continue into next year. I am also confident I can continue to make the necessary changes to increase retention. Clients are finding us of their own accord and requesting our services. There is a process that takes less time. The cost of acquiring a new customer will begin to trend down as well. It is for these reasons that I would like a raise."

"Yes, Amira." Mr. McAlister cleared his throat. "You have been a great asset. Your growth over the last year has been impressive. How long have you been here? Two years?"

"Almost three, sir."

"Yes! That's right. Yes, this company has benefited from the great teamwork we have here. I am not in charge of raises. Our finance department does that. But the yearly salary increase reflects the company's growth. I am positive the raise this year will show that."

"The annual increase is appreciated, but I am requesting a raise specifically for me. I've done a market analysis of my position, and I am under the average salary for the area. My education, ideas, and leadership have helped the company significantly. I would like to be making above average. The results from my work this year show I can create profits, and an increase would be an investment."

"As I said, raises and salaries are decided by the finance department. They have their payroll and ultimately, they would decide if it fit into the budget. From there, it would go to HR to be approved. I don't have the final say on those kinds of matters."

"I understand. Would you be willing to put in a recommendation for me? I have a proposal letter I can provide you. It has the current market analysis for my position based on my experience and education. It also has the salary I am requesting and the contributions I have made this year. I can provide you with a copy to keep as well. I have extras." Amira handed him the papers. The slight shift in his smile and eyes indicated he didn't want to take them, but did anyway. She put on a smile of her own. "Thank you so much. I appreciate it."

"Not a problem," he said, recovering. "I can submit this, but I can't make any promises. It is out of my control."

"I understand. When can I expect a response back?"

"You would like to hear back from someone?"

"Yes, I'd like to know it was considered. I know people are busy, and I wouldn't want it to end up lost on someone's desk."

"They are very responsible in finance. I am sure they won't lose it. But again, it isn't my department. I can't speak on when it would be addressed or if someone is able to reach out to you. But I can assure you, the raises we have rolling out this year will reflect the great teamwork we have here."

Amira took a brief pause and kept her smile skillfully across her face. She had asked for a raise and was told she would receive the company one. She would still be under market and behind her coworkers. There was no promise or guarantee that her proposal letter would make it to the finance department. Or that someone would notify her it was received. Without any form of confirmation, she had no idea how long she would be waiting for a response. Her pink and red polka-dot umbrella popped into her mind. *Fuck it.* She didn't expect an answer at this meeting, but she was looking for assurance that it would be addressed in a timely manner. That wasn't provided. She had hoped she wouldn't have to do this next step, but decided it was now necessary.

"Mr. McAlister, I have another company offering significantly more salary with equal benefits. I do like working here. It's a wonderful environment. That's why I came to you. I would love this company to match the offer I received. They are asking me to reply by next week. I would need a response from our finance department by the end of this week. If I don't hear from them, I will have to assume the answer is no. Is it possible for someone to notify me that my request was received? Even if it is an email?"

Mr. McAlister's smile dropped. His eyes masked over, carefully hiding his emotions. Amira wasn't able to read him. "I'm sorry you are thinking of leaving us. I can relay everything you provided, along with your letter. It will still be the finance department that determines whether the budget allows for this salary or not. You should consider waiting until the annual raise is announced. It should be coming out in the next couple of weeks."

"It wasn't an easy choice to start looking elsewhere. I am hoping I won't have to leave."

"Yes. Yes, me too. Well, I will give them your information. Anything else you would like to discuss while we are here?"

"No, thank you Mr. McAlister. I appreciate your taking the time to listen." Amira said as she stood.

"I'll see you at the afternoon staff meeting."

Amira checked in with him on Wednesday in passing to ask if he had an update. He said he didn't. There was nothing in her inbox. Her stomach was in knots all week. She alternated between being proud and wondering if she had fucked everything up. Friday afternoon she received an email from finance with her boss cc'd. It discussed how they valued her as an employee and appreciated her contributions. However, at this time the company would not be able to accommodate her request. They stated that it would be up for evaluation again next fiscal year if she continued her current work ethic. In the meantime, this year's across the board raise was going to be higher than in previous years.

Amira took the weekend to think about it. Her male coworkers would still be earning more than her. The new woman hired this year was still making more than she would. She didn't like that she had to keep pushing for an answer. If there was enough money for a higher across the board raise, how was there not enough to bring her salary up to the market average? She wasn't even given a counteroffer, just told no. It was a consideration for next year. She asked for what she wanted. She didn't get it.

On Monday, she sent one email to the new company accepting the offer and one to Mr. McAlister with her two weeks' notice.

Rita: Age 32

Rita climbed out of the car, opened the trunk, and grabbed all six grocery bags. She waddled up the steps, her breath heavy, bags knocking at her legs as the weight pulled her arms down. Her purse slid off her shoulder and threatened to trip her. The outside light was off. She had gotten out of work late and hadn't planned to come home in the dark. She fumbled to unlock the door and shoved it open with her shoulder, dropping everything on the mudroom floor with a sigh. Rita flicked the light on and was greeted by laundry piled in the hamper. It was the same dirty load that she had brought down this morning. A quick check confirmed that wet laundry was still in the washer and the clothes in the dryer were cold and slightly damp.

After restarting the dryer and picking up all the groceries, she lumbered into the kitchen. The volume of the television assaulted her ears. An open pizza box had been left on the small counter with one slice remaining. The cheese was cold and congealed. She didn't try to guess how many hours it had been sitting out. Dishes with dried food and empty soda cans were tossed in the sink. Rita congratulated herself on at least remembering to start the dishwasher before she left, despite knowing intuitively they were still in there. While putting away groceries, she discovered the leftovers she had placed on a plate in the fridge were untouched. Her shoulders fell, and another sigh escaped her lips.

By the time the dryer alarm went off, the groceries were put away and most of the kitchen was cleaned. She switched the laundry and grabbed the clothes to fold in the living room. John was sitting on the couch watching a basketball game. On the coffee table in front of him sat a plate with a half-eaten piece of pizza, a takeout container filled with chicken bones, and another can of soda.

"Where you been?" he asked. His eyes narrowed as he alternated between giving her a side-eye and not wanting to miss the action on the television.

"I've been home for a while now. You didn't hear me?"

"Nah. But you shoulda been home."

"I got out of work late and still had to go grocery shopping."

John cut his eyes to her and grunted.

"I noticed you bought pizza and wings instead of heating up the plate of food I left for you," she said cautiously.

"Rita, you know I don't eat leftovers like that."

"Your job has been sending you home early. We don't know when you will start getting your full-time hours again. We've gotta be smart with how we spend money."

"So, I'm stupid because I ordered food for the first time in a month?" he sneered.

"John, you just ordered out last week." The comment was met with another sideways glance. "I made extra yesterday because today was a double. All you had to do was put the plate in the microwave."

"I'm not gonna argue with you about this. I'm still bringing home a paycheck and can spend my money however the fuck I want to," he said vehemently.

Rita fell silent and turned her attention to the laundry. John's eyes stopped cutting to her and focused on the television, as he turned the volume up a little louder. She retreated to the kitchen as soon as the laundry was folded to finish cleaning. When the dryer alarmed again, she threw the last load in and took the laundry upstairs to fold in the bedroom. With some distance between her and the living room, her shoulders began to relax. Rita massaged her neck and her temples, but the throbbing headache did not ease. She could usually relax when all the chores were done, but tonight the tension lingered. She popped ibuprofen while the shower water got hot. Steam filled the bathroom, and the mirror fogged. She climbed in and let the water hit her back, burning and tinting her skin red. Rita breathed in the steam, rubbing her neck and shoulders again, massaging the knots out. Stepping out, she rubbed cocoa butter across the stretch marks on her thighs, belly, and breasts. She slipped into an oversized, stained t-shirt and lounge pants with frayed ends. The mirror was still fogged, but she didn't need it. The heavy-set face in the mirror was one she tried to avoid.

She crawled into bed, curling on her side. The glow from her phone mocked her with the late hour. Closing her eyes, she took deep breaths to encourage sleep. The TV clicked off in the living room. John's heavy footsteps were on the stairs, and she listened as he walked to the bathroom. Her shoulders tightened, but she kept her eyes closed and tried to breathe evenly.

He pulled the covers back, the bed creaking as he got in. He wrapped his arms around her and pressed his body against her back.

"Listen, Rita, I'm sorry I snapped. I just wanted to do something nice for myself. I never get to do anything I want. Besides, I could be out drinkin' at the bar. The guys at work invited me out. Instead, I came home and ate pizza and wings. Why you got such an attitude?" John's syrupy voice held a defensive tone.

Rita felt his dick on her ass through her pajamas. "I'm tired, John. I want to go to sleep."

"You come home and don't say anything to me. You yelled because I didn't eat leftovers when you know I don't eat that shit. We didn't get any time together tonight. I wanna spend some time with you."

"I didn't yell. You didn't notice I was home the entire time I cleaned the kitchen. You've been here for hours and left the laundry and the dishes. Food was left out on the counter. Food was in the living room. I got out late. I have a headache, and I want to go to sleep."

"You don't have to do anything. Just lie there."

"I have work in the morning, John. I want to go to bed."

"I gotta work, too. I gotta be up earlier'n you. You know this helps me sleep better."

"If you can't sleep, go downstairs and watch TV. Maybe you'll fall asleep on the couch again."

"Really, Rita? So you can yell at me tomorrow when I'm late for my job because I couldn't sleep? You haven't fucked me in over a week. I'm not even askin' you to be on top. Just lie there. I'll do all the work." He pushed his dick harder against her ass. "Just lie on your back. That's all you gotta do." A sigh accidentally slipped from Rita. "Oh, so now you gonna start sighin' and shit? Because I want to give you love?"

Rita rolled onto her back. She knew he wouldn't stop talking, wouldn't stop bothering her, wouldn't stop rubbing his dick against her ass until she gave in. John pulled down his boxer shorts. "Take your pants off while you suck it. Get it harder." Rita obeyed. John grabbed her hair, using it to shove her head up and down. "That's better." He paused to slap her ass. "Keep going. I'll tell you when you can lie down."

Rita had no concept of time. It always felt like forever when this happened. Eventually, he told her to lie on her back, and he rolled on top of her. He spat on his hand, slapped it against her pussy, and shoved his dick inside her. The sting from the friction tears made her breath intake sharply. She held her breath, trying to be quiet and still. The bed rocked back and forth as he shoved himself inside her as fast as he could. His body hit against hers. Smack. Smack. Smack.

"I love this pussy," he groaned between his loud, labored breathing. Enough light streamed from the window for Rita to see the sweat beads on his forehead. His face contorted as he watched his dick go in and out of her. When his arms couldn't hold himself up anymore, he laid on top of her. It hurt less at this angle, but the weight and closeness of his body was worse than the pain from sex.

"Open your legs more, Rita. Those thighs of yours are gettin' bigger, gettin' in the way. Take your shirt off, too. I wanna see them titties. I like them big." John pushed himself up. Rita took off her shirt and tried to open her legs more through the tightness in her hips.

John stared at her chest as he shoved himself into her. Smack. Smack. Smack. He moved faster, the bed rocking violently. Rita gripped the bedsheets and muffled her cries. She knew he was almost done. She just had to lie still a little longer. She couldn't look at his face anymore, twisted as it was, in concentration and pride. He thought fucking her as hard and as fast as possible was good sex. She had told him in the past that it hurt. It never stopped him. Rita stared at the ceiling, waiting. Soon, he bellowed as he came, pumping a few more times before falling on top of her. He remained until his heavy breathing subsided, rolled off her, turned the TV on, and crawled under the covers.

"See. I told you, you'd just have to lie there," he said.

Rita stood up to go to the bathroom, his stickiness running down her thighs. Her body was sore, tender, and tight. She cleaned up, put her pajamas back on, and got into bed. She placed herself as close to the edge as possible and curled up on her side. She almost checked her phone to find out what time it was. Sometimes it lasted five minutes; sometimes it lasted longer. Tonight, she didn't have the willpower to check the time.

Annie: Age 38

Annie couldn't have picked a better day to go to the pumpkin patch. The sky was bright blue with thin, wispy clouds against brightly colored trees. It was pleasantly warm, and a slight breeze carried delightful autumn smells. Her son, Elijah, didn't want to come. He was at the age where he proclaimed pumpkin patches were stupid. He was too old for them. However, Annie knew that he still had a lot of fun when he got there.

She chose one that had the atmosphere of a fair. There was a section to shoot basketballs, toss baseballs, throw footballs, and clock pitching speed. Hay bales were built into forts to run through or pyramids to climb on. Kids could play in kernels and stick their heads in a hole over a silly body. The side of the hill had been turned into a huge slide. A beat-up, makeshift mini-golf course was in the center of the area and tires and ropes had been formed an obstacle course. Cornhole was next to an inflatable bounce house. Concession stands were at the front and back of the field. One side had the entrance to the corn maze, and the opposite area had the wagon ride pulled by a tractor to the pumpkin patch. Farm animals and a small petting zoo were next to a corral where horse and pony rides were available for an extra fee. Elijah would find something enjoyable here. That was why she chose this one despite similar fall festivals closer to home. Instead, Annie drove a little farther and spent a little more to go to the nicer patch that would have something her son would like.

The two of them had already explored half of the amusements when they reached the back, where apple launchers were set up. "Want to try?" She asked, nodding her head towards them.

He shrugged. "Sure. Why not?"

There was an additional fee to launch apples, and the line was longer here than anywhere else. When it was their turn, they climbed up the platform and grabbed a bucket of ten. The fruit was small and reminded Annie of the wild apples from her childhood. The air-powered cannon was large and cumbersome. Elijah needed help loading and aiming it at the target. At first, they completely missed it. Gradually, they improved and got closer to hitting the bullseye. After the bucket was empty, he talked excitedly about how close he got to the center.

They had to wait in a couple more lines after the launcher, but they moved faster. Everyone wanted to go down the zipline and the slide against the hillside. Getting into the corn maze was no trouble, but finding a way out proved much harder. They got turned around and had to backtrack multiple times. After conquering that, Elijah grabbed her arm and pulled her into the kiddie maze. The goat race happened when Annie was waiting in the concession line buying lunch. Elijah was playing in the bounce house and didn't care that he missed it. She wished she had seen it. Instead, they took extra time at the petting zoo. Elijah asked for hot cocoa and cookies. She said to wait until they were leaving since the cookie stall was at the entrance.

Last was the wagon ride to the field. Her son promptly picked a huge orange pumpkin and carried it himself. Annie treated herself to two. One was smaller and white. The second was odd-shaped and greenish with large bumps. They placed them on a scale, and she paid per pound. After five hours, they were exhausted. The beautiful fall day had turned chilly. They were cold, hungry, and tired. As they hauled the pumpkins to the car, Elijah reminded her about the cocoa and cookies.

"Are you sure you want to go back in?" she asked.

"I really want to go home. But I have enough energy to go back."

After dropping off the pumpkins, they walked back to the entrance. After standing in another line, they found out the cookies were sold out and only apple cider donuts were left. Annie bought two, along with hot cocoa and hot cider. Elijah took a tentative bite, his eyes widening. He exclaimed through a full mouth that he had not expected to like it.

"I really needed this, Mom. This makes me feel so much better."

"I really needed it, too."

Annie sipped her cider as she drove home. Memories of picking apples and hanging out in her tree fort came back to her. She recalled sitting at a table in college, drizzling free honey on an apple. Now here she was. She'd taken Elijah to the more expensive pumpkin patch and paid by the pound for pumpkins. She was able to afford food at concession stands, and had even stood in line again to buy donuts. She did a mental tally in her head, adding up the expenses for these few hours with Elijah. It was an old habit developed over years of surviving and rebuilding. She'd lost everything in the bankruptcy, but rebuilt it after going back to school. Now, in the middle of a divorce, she needed to rebuild again. She'd spent so much time trying to create a happy life with her son and husband. She'd spent so much time trying to stop it from falling apart. Now, she was attempting to establish something different, alone. She had to create a life as a single mother and create a new relationship with her son.

Elijah set up the music playlist and relaxed into the warm car. He looked at the clock and was surprised at how fast time had passed. He didn't realize he could still have so much fun at a pumpkin patch. Annie smiled at him, told him she was glad he enjoyed himself, and said she liked it, too. She took a mental tally of the cost and reviewed her budget in her head. She realized with surprise that she could afford today. It had been worth it to keep trying.

She glanced at her son. In a few years, he would be a teenager. He wouldn't want to do things with her, especially an activity like this. He would want to be with friends and to go out with them. He would be busy with sports. Her tally left her mind. The cost didn't matter. This moment with Elijah was worth so much more than money.

Rita: Age 38

Rita turned on her fun, relaxing playlist. It was the only thing she could think of to calm her nerves as she drove to Travis's house. It was her first time going to his place, but her fifth in-person date with him. She'd started texting him two months ago and spent the last month seeing him on casual, weekly dates. She hadn't expected online dating to work in real life. In fact, for the first year and a half, it didn't. In-app messaging was rough and awkward. In person, it did not sail any smoother. Rita kept trying, hoping something would work out even for a brief period. The divorce from John had been long and messy. Anxiety had left her body thirty pounds lighter. Her lawyer and therapist had left her bank account thousands of dollars lighter. The number of double shifts she worked to make ends meet kept her sleep deprived. For almost two years after finalizing the divorce, she couldn't bring herself to do much of anything. It was sheer force of will that got her to start dating again.

Travis was not the sort of man she would normally date. He was a few years younger than her, with defined muscles covered in tattoos and a head he shaved because of a receding hairline. He was not the image that came to mind when someone said "corporate accountant." He had shown up for a couple of dates on his motorcycle since the weather turned sunny. He looked great in a leather jacket. She never thought she would hang out with a guy who wore leather. She hadn't thought a biker would be interested in her, especially not a younger one.

When she liked him in the app, she thought it was a shot in the dark. She hadn't expected him to respond.

Then, she hadn't expected him to keep talking to her. She thought he would lose interest when they met in person. Each message she received after a date surprised her. Each text with an insightful question, sarcastic remark, or sincere affection left her stunned. He volunteered his time helping people prepare their tax returns. He was an avid hiker and an amateur photographer. She re-read messages and replayed conversations in her head trying to uncover something wrong with him. Ironically, it scared her that she didn't notice any obvious red flags. However, it terrified her to go to his place. It had been over a decade since Rita had gone to a man's house for a date.

The weekend before, she had gone shopping for a new set of matching bra and underwear. Nothing she owned was pretty. John hadn't paid attention to anything she'd worn in years. She picked up condoms, just in case, and spent an hour attempting to find an outfit that looked nice without trying to look nice. Rita's head spun the entire time she put on different clothes. She alternated between scolding herself for trying so hard and lecturing herself for not having casually dressy clothing to wear. In the end, she chose the comfortable jeans that were snug and showed off her curves but stopped her belly from hanging over. She found a black V-neck shirt in the back of her closet. She remembered wearing it several years ago before she gained weight and must have forgotten to donate it when it had become too small. Now, it was slightly too big and plunged a little lower than she anticipated. That was another problem with all her clothes. Nothing fit. The unexpected thirty-pound weight loss had jump-started a health journey of intentional fitness. While that left her energy level the highest it had been in years, it also left her clothing loose and saggy. The jeans were a new buy from a thrift store. She had gotten tired of continuously pulling her pants up and adding holes to belts.

Dressing for the first two dates with Travis had been very difficult. She was starting to become comfortable and think less about how she dressed around him. However, the visit to his house instigated her over-analyzing again. On the spur-of-the-moment, she applied light makeup. She hadn't worn it since their first date, and her skill level in this area was almost nonexistent. She'd stopped wearing makeup on dates a year ago since most first dates didn't lead to a second. Before she started dating, it had been years since she had put anything on her face. Travis was bringing out a new side.

Her GPS showed a ten-minute estimated arrival time. Large houses pressed down on her. These were the kind of homes that had finished basements and extra rooms used for playrooms, crafts, exercise, or offices. Attached decks with outdoor furniture sets had steps leading down to patios with grills. Half of the yards were fenced in with pools. She recognized Mercedes, Telsas, and Mustangs parked next to minivans with stick figure families on the back window. Rita swallowed hard and willed her heart to stop beating so fast.

She saw his Harley Davidson before her GPS notified her she had arrived. His house was slightly smaller than the others on the block. The yard was well kept with a grill and smoker but not fenced and had no pool. She carefully parked next to the bike and noticed the SUV inside his garage. She took slow, easy breaths as she walked up to the front door and rang the doorbell.

Travis opened the door wearing a huge smile, his eyes bright. He pulled her into a light embrace, swiftly closing the door behind her. "I don't want Burtie and Eartha to get out." As if on cue, a black cat with a white patch on the nose and paw trotted down the hall. "That's Eartha. Don't touch her yet. You've gotta give her time to warm up to you. She's fierce when she wants to be and quick to try to escape. Burtie is the lazy one. She's probably on the back of the couch sunbathing."

"Those are strange names for cats. I didn't know you had pets."

"Shit. You aren't allergic, are you?" he asked nervously. Rita shook her head, and Travis's face relaxed again. "A friend was finding homes for her cat's litter. I picked these two out when they were young. It was a play on Burt and Ernie, except it turns out the one I was calling Burt wasn't a boy. At that point, the name stuck. I knew Eartha was a girl. She's named after Eartha Kitt. Eartha's meow isn't a normal cat meow. Come into the kitchen. I was planning on grilling us something. Your choice."

His house was clean and open, with plenty of natural lighting. Landscape photographs and abstract art decorated the downstairs. An instrumental beat played in the background. It was the type of noise designed to create focus and loud enough to break the silence. He opened his fridge full of fresh fruits and vegetables, burgers, steaks, and sausages. Rita chose sausage with peppers and onions. Travis cut up tomatoes, lettuce, and onions for his burger. He offered her wine, which she declined, opting for water instead.

She helped him carry the food out to the deck. His easy chatter as he grilled put her at ease. Their conversation flowed from one topic to the next, mixed with laughter and soft jabs. As the sun lowered, a chilly air set in.

"I love this weather," he said. "Summer is so fucking hot. But now? Warm days aren't so hot and humid. Cool nights make sleep easier. I don't like that it gets darker sooner. That fucking sucks for sure. But the time right before fall starts to become too cold is the best. You wanna go inside? You seem cold."

Rita nodded and helped him take care of the food

and dishes. "You can leave them on the counter. Have a seat at the table. I'm gonna rinse them off and throw them in the dishwasher."

"I can help put them away."

"You're not gonna do anything but keep me company. Or you can eat dessert. Are you interested in dessert?" Rita shook her head. It didn't take Travis long to clean up. He started the dishwasher, walked over and pulled her up from her chair, wrapping his arms around her. She paused, then embraced him back. "Am I making you uncomfortable right now?" he asked softly.

"No."

"Rita, I would love it if you came upstairs to my room. I don't know if that's too much too fast, but there's no way in hell I can let you leave without at least asking."

"I'd like that."

Travis tilted her head up and kissed her lips, took her hand, and led her upstairs. He removed her shirt, kissing her neck and breasts. She tried to take off his shirt, but he moved her arms down to her side. His fingers darted to her zipper and pulled her pants down. He kissed her belly and thighs as he took off each article of clothing. Rita attempted to strip him again. Standing still as he gave her stretched skin intimate attention was unnerving. Travis clasped her wrists, stopped her a second time, and stood up. He pressed against her barely clothed figure until the bed was against the back of her legs. Suddenly, her feet were off the floor as he picked her up and placed her on the mattress.

"You don't have to do anything right now. Just lie on your back. That's all you've gotta do." He pulled her underwear off. "I didn't think you were a lace-lingerie kind of girl."

"I'm not." Rita said it so faintly it was almost a whisper. Her body tensed.

"Did you wear them for me?"

She nodded, cheeks burning. She turned her head away from him. Travis climbed on top of her, taking her wrists and moving them above her head. One hand held both of her wrists down. His other hand tilted her head towards him, gently kissing her neck. His lips shifted to her forehead, then cheek until his mouth was on hers. He kissed her until she relaxed, then deepened his kiss, sliding his tongue inside. His free hand moved from her face down her body, caressing it. A sigh escaped Rita's mouth, and the tension left her.

"They look real good on you." Travis kissed her chest, moving her bra down to suck her nipple. He covered it up to switch to the other breast, giving that nipple equal attention before placing the fabric back in place and trailing kisses farther down. His hands hooked her panties and tugged them. Rita sharply inhaled as Travis buried his face in between her legs, licking the inside of her pussy. He slid in a finger, taking his time. "But I don't need you to wear them if you don't want to. You look good without them. Taste and smell good, too." Travis's tongue went back inside her, moving in and out like his fingers had been doing a moment ago. He licked up, found her clit and made light circles and flicks with his tongue. His finger delved back in, priming her more before adding a second.

Rita alternated between squeezing her eyes tight as pleasure overwhelmed her and watching him feast. She was stunned to discover she liked to watch him devour her. Embarrassment made her turn her head. But Travis would do something with his tongue or his finger, and she would cry out. Her body arched, and she threw her head back. Her embarrassment vanished as waves of new sensations swept over her. The pleasure was intense. Rita's legs closed up, and she shifted away from him. Travis's eyes shot up and locked with hers. His arms slid under her thighs, pulling her back to him, deeper into his mouth. His hands pushed her legs slowly open, trailing his fingers across her inner thighs before sliding them inside her, this time with more aggression and force. Rita cried out, eyes shut tight as the orgasm she wasn't prepared for hit her. His tongue moved away from her clit to her pussy, darting inside her.

She tried to move, but Travis's arms clasped her hips in place. "I'm not done yet. You're going to keep lying there."

"But I came."

He smirked. "I know. I heard you. I felt you. I tasted you. But I'm not done yet."

Then his mouth was sucking her clit, tongue teasing against it. The sensation was extreme, and she twisted and wiggled. His grip tightened, pushing her hips into the bed. Rita couldn't turn away, even when they locked eyes and watched each other. Her breathing became heavier. Travis shifted his weight, using one arm to keep her pinned to the bed and the other to thrust his fingers inside her. More moans escaped her lips. His fingers moved faster as he sucked harder, the ecstasy building up. The next time his eyes met hers, Rita exploded. Her cries came out so loud she didn't recognize them as hers. Gushes shot out of her. He moaned against her pussy, eyes focused on her as she came again. His tongue kept flicking against her clit. Rita's thighs clamped shut. Her legs crossed behind his head, and her hips arched. He simply moved his face up with her body and supported her lower back with his arms. A third orgasm washed over her. Her moans dropped low and rough, and her breathing was heavy as she shook. Travis chuckled as his tongue slowed, lapping her up.

When he was done, he lowered her hips back down and took off his clothes. Rita had almost caught her breath, but seeing his muscles and size made it quicken. Her eyes widened. She glanced up at Travis's face, checking if he noticed her reaction. He smiled.

"I won't hurt you. I promise. And if it gets uncomfortable, tell me. I can slow down or stop if you need me to." She could only nod. "Come here. Suck it. Take off your bra when you do it."

Rita rolled onto her knees to take off her bra. His eyes turned dark as her breasts fell out. His eyes alternated between her face and her chest, undecided where the best place to stare was. She placed her hands on the bed to move towards Travis.

"Yes, crawl over here. Crawl over to me," he commanded. His face was intense.

Rita froze, wondering if she had heard him correctly. He leaned closer to her, softly kissing her lips. His hand ran down her spine, massaging it until the tension left her body. He pulled away, smiling. Her body arched and her ass curved into the air as she crawled towards Travis. She wanted his dick in her mouth. She couldn't remember the last time she had wanted to do this. She grabbed his cock, jacking it off as she leaned forward to suck it.

"Wait," he said. Rita's eyebrows creased with concern. "Do you want me to wear a condom for this?"

"Umm. No. No. Not really." Rita stammered, surprised by her response. She knew the risks, and that it wasn't smart. She knew they hadn't discussed whether they were going to be monogamous or not. She understood that that was not the answer she should give. He seemed to be able to tell, too.

"Are you sure?"

She paused for a second to re-evaluate. Her eyes moved down to his dick. "Yes. Yes, I am sure."

He smirked again. "I am going to wear one when I fuck you. I have a condom in the nightstand drawer. How about you crawl over and grab one? It'll give me the chance to look at that ass naked." Rita obeyed. She glanced over her shoulder as she crawled. Travis stared at her ass, rubbing his cock with his hand. Her pussy tingled and throbbed in anticipation. On a split-second decision, she brought the condom back to him, holding the wrapper with her teeth, deliberately moving slowly. Travis stroked her cheek and took the condom. "Good girl. Suck it. Get it harder. I'll tell you when you can lie down."

Rita licked him up and down before taking him into her mouth. She worked her way down, but not quite all the way to the back of her throat. Travis placed his hand on the back of her head, and she sucked faster, her tongue licking his shaft. His hand tightened, using her hair to control her movements. She grabbed his bare ass, dug her nails in and pulled him closer to her face. Another moan escaped, muffled by his dick in her throat. Rita had no concept of time as Travis controlled her depth and speed. When she tried to take more initiative, he tugged her hair, maintaining authority.

"One day, Rita, I want to fuck your mouth, but not today. Turn around. Put your ass in the air."

Travis spread her ass cheeks, his tongue quickly finding her clit and his thumb pressing around her asshole. Rita sharply inhaled at the new, unexpectedly enjoyable sensation. A sudden sting from the slap of his hand against her pussy startled her, and she cried out. His finger slid in, then a second, then a third. The alternating pressure from her pussy and asshole made her legs quiver. She heard the condom wrapper tear, then her lips stretched as Travis gingerly penetrated her. He paused to allow her body to relax into him. His pace started soft as he moved in and out, but as his breathing increased so did his speed. Smack. His hand hit one ass cheek, then the other. Smack. Smack. Smack. Rita cried out, her body sinking into the bed, bringing her ass up higher in the air.

His thumb stayed on her asshole, pressing. His dick shoved inside her, faster, harder. Rita held her breath and tried to be quiet and still, but a yelp escaped.

Travis stopped. "Rita, are you okay?"

"Umm. Yeah. I'm okay."

"Are you sure?"

"Well. It… it's kinda a lot."

"What part is a lot? Or is it all too much?"

"Your… your dick. It's a lot. From the back. I like it. It was just starting to hurt a little. It's okay. You can keep going."

"Roll onto your back. We can try a different position and see if that helps. I'll slow down, too. And not go as deep."

Rita rolled over and Travis crawled on top of her, guiding his dick back inside and wrapping an arm around her, pulling her close. The weight and closeness of his body made her relax into the bed.

"Open your legs up more. Let me in between those thick thighs. Good girl." Travis kissed her neck, his fingers pinching her nipple. "I'm gonna like seeing you on your back, too," he whispered in her ear, sending shivers down her spine. "I can watch and play with your tits."

His mouth took her breast in, sucking hard and lightly biting. Rita's head shot back. Her eyes closed and mouth dropped. Her legs opened, allowing him more access. Travis took a steady pace, the length of him sliding in and out. Yet he didn't completely enter her. The anticipation of feeling him deep in her core became stronger than she could resist. She ran her hands down his back and grabbed his ass, lifting her hips up as she tried to push him further in.

"Rita, I don't want to hurt you."

"I… I like it. I want more."

He chuckled. "Lift your hips up." He set pillows under her ass to tilt her pelvis up. He stood at the edge of the bed and slid his dick back inside. "Tell me if it's too much, okay?" She nodded. He started out slowly to give her time to adjust to the new angle. Gradually, he increased his speed and depth. Rita gripped the bedsheets, crying out with each thrust. "Do you like this?" he asked, his voice husky.

"Yes."

Travis started rubbing her clit, causing more moans to escape. "You don't have to be quiet if you don't want to. I like your noise. I'm gonna like watching you come on my dick, too."

"Harder. Please, harder."

His intensity elevated, his finger rubbing her clit and his thumb going back to her asshole, pressing. He watched his dick go in and out of her, hunger and focus across his face. She exploded, her pussy clenching his cock. Travis kept going, and another wave followed. His pace slowed again until he stopped, eyes dark and compelling. With a smile across his lips, he crawled on top of her again, kissing her neck. "Good girl." He murmured in her ear. "Brace yourself, okay?"

"Okay," she said, barely audible.

Travis placed his hand on her collarbone. Rita was so wet his dick moved smoothly back inside her. He started fiercely fucking her, her legs falling open for him. Smack. Smack. Smack. She took his hand from her collarbone, moving it up higher on her neck. His focused expression studied her face for any signs of distress. It unnerved her. She had to close her eyes. Travis kept his hand firmly wrapped around her neck, yet never squeezing. His mouth sucked and bit her nipples again before leaning against her ear.

"The condom is still on. I want to come in you."

"Yes. Yes." Her hands gripped his shoulders. She dug her nails into his back, lifting her hips for deeper penetration. His powerful thrusts had her crying out. He moaned, his body quivered as he rested on top of her, catching his breath. Travis didn't stay long, choosing instead to wrap his arms around her. He shifted onto his back, pulling her against his side. Rita rested her head on his shoulder, a happy sigh slipping out.

Travis smirked. "I told you, you would just have to lie there." Rita smiled. He cleared his throat. "I need to apologize. I didn't plan on doing all of that. I planned on keeping it simple for the first time and then seeing what you were comfortable with. I got caught up."

"I… ummm… I liked it."

"I thought so. That's why I kept going," he said as he rubbed her back.

"Is that what you prefer?"

"Yeah. Things like that. Or more intense. Is that something you might be okay with?"

"Yeah. Yeah, I think I'd like to find out how much I am okay with."

"Do you know what you like?"

"No. Not really. Not anymore."

Travis kissed her forehead. "If you think of anything you may like, you can tell me."

"Okay."

"Are you interested in dessert now?" He smiled at her. "I picked up strawberry cheesecake. You ordered it once when we went out. I thought it would be the safest dessert to have."

"I love strawberry cheesecake."

"It's too late for me to drink coffee. But I can make some if you want. Or tea. Or wine."

"Tea. I love tea in the evening." Rita said.

Travis rolled out of bed. "You can use my master bath if you need to. I'll be in the kitchen."

Rita stood up, her body loose and relaxed. She rubbed her shoulders trying to find knots and was surprised to find none. After cleaning up and getting dressed, she met him downstairs. Two cups of tea and cheesecake were on the table. She was again surprised at how easy the conversation continued and how they both ended up laughing. The outside darkness prompted her to check her phone, the glowing time indicating she'd stayed much longer than planned. Travis kissed her goodbye, holding her close as she held him back.

Rita's drive home was spent thinking about him. She headed to the bathroom and leisurely stood in front of the mirror, removing her makeup. After her face was clean, she hopped in the shower, letting the hot water hit her and the steam fill the room. She noticed a small bite mark on her nipple and smiled, wishing there were more. She filed the thought away to think about later. As she was getting into her pajamas, her phone notification sounded. Travis had messaged. "Wanted to make sure you got home okay."

She replied. "I did. Thanks again for having me over."

Travis quickly responded. "I really hope you will come over again."

Cassandra: Age 41

I pull the blanket up a little more and snuggle deeper into the couch, slowly sipping coffee. My phone is out, so I'm taking screenshots for documentation. The lawyer advised me to "document, document, document." A couple of friends who went through nasty divorces already told me to do the same thing. "Document everything!" When I started, that was very vague. What is everything? What is important? What if I miss something? Where am I supposed to keep this? It took months, but I created a system, and I've learned to make this time a little easier over the last year. I do this every week. It keeps me from having to remember too far back and find things. It took a while to figure out how often to document as well. I tried daily and was overwhelmed. I tried whenever I had time and kept forgetting where I left off. Sometimes it was looking back a couple of days, sometimes a couple weeks. Now, I schedule this time weekly. It's a much smoother process.

It's the text messages I am screenshotting right now. I like to wait timestamp. My phone says "yesterday" or "Monday." I wait for the actual date to appear. Maybe there's a way to change it so the date is always visible. If there is, I don't have the brain capacity to figure it out. I have no clue if or when I will need these text messages. I email the mean and angry texts to my lawyer. Sometimes I receive a response; sometimes I don't. I try not to send her a lot of emails. Each one I send and receive is charged against my retainer. Some of the text messages are mundane but turn out to be important later. His story changes. He lies to me. He tells me he didn't say things that he did. He tells me he said things that he didn't. He tells me I didn't provide him with information when I did. I don't call him out every time he lies. I save it for court. Or, I find peace in knowing I am not crazy or imagining it. He is lying to me. If he does decide to pay child support for the month or half of our agreed-upon expenses, he sends it electronically. I screenshot that as well.

It's gotten easier to screenshot messages. I text him less. "Keep it short. Keep it professional. Don't fall for the bait. Wait before replying if you need to. Don't text anything you wouldn't want a judge to see. Avoid talking on the phone or in person. If you do, send a message stating what was discussed and when." This is the advice I've received from friends, from my lawyer, and from the mediator. If we happen to talk on the phone, I take a screenshot showing the time and length of the conversation. It was overwhelming at first, but I got the hang of it.

Next are his social media accounts. Unfortunately, I must do those twice. He can delete them whenever. I take screenshots of every post as soon as I notice it. Then, I take screenshots of dated posts. I end up with duplicate pictures. But he's deleted posts occasionally, and I have proof of it. I'm lucky we don't send each other emails. All the emails my lawyer sends me are in a separate folder. After social media accounts, I open the team communication apps. I have told him several times that he needs to download these apps. Sometimes he does; sometimes he doesn't. I take pictures of the game and practice schedule and any changes that happen. If he is on the app, I screenshot all the new messages. If he isn't, I screenshot the roster of parents to prove he still isn't on the app. When coaches text in group chats, I take a picture. Along with any texts that teachers send. He is on the children's school form as a contact, and he has sent me questions based on teachers' message. That's how I can tell he receives them. There is also a group chat between the daycare and both of us. That gets screenshot as well.

My coworker told me her mother-in-law was a huge help during her divorce. Her mother-in-law saved pictures of the conversations between her and her son, then gave them to her to use in court. She knew her son wasn't a fit father. She helped to make sure her grandchildren were in a safe environment. I don't have that. My parents-in-law also say terrible things about me to my children.

I screenshot any pictures I sent him. Again, a little redundant. I end up with duplicates. But my phone puts screenshots in a separate folder. It makes the overall organization easier for me. He likes to say I never tell him about the children. He likes to say he didn't know about school events or doctor's visits or grades or games and practices. I tell him when the school calendar is available. I send him pictures of all the flyers and papers the children bring home. I send him their report cards. I send him receipts of extracurricular expenses, medical costs, lunch and education costs. Whatever else happened with the kids in the last week. I take a picture of the big announcement boards in front of their schools. It says the dates when the school has early dismissals or is closed. He has to drop the children off. He can read the sign.

The oldest child has a phone. I take pictures of what he texts her. He has said terrible things about me to my oldest. He says I am trying to take her away. That I am brainwashing her and lying to her. He says I am a bitch who is doing this for money. That I destroyed our family. He asks her questions about what I do to trick her into spying on me. He uses her as the middle person to relay information instead of communicating directly to me. He discusses what was said in mediation and twists it out of context to make himself look good. I'm sure what he tells all three children in person is worse. I think he figured out that I check her phone. He doesn't text her as often, but I know he still says mean and inappropriate things about me.

Last for now are the GPS trackers I place in the children's backpacks. He's picked them up late, or not arrived at all. That's the reason for taking pictures of the announcement board. I have received calls from the principal that the children were waiting to be picked up and he wasn't answering his phone. When that happens, I screenshot the phone call from the school and send a text to him. If a message was left, I save it. I have a folder of saved voicemail messages. I've gotten several nasty voicemails from him.

The other reason for the GPS is that he is lying about where he lives. My youngest let it slip that Daddy had moved. When I confronted him about it, he denied it. He said his girlfriend moved, but he is in the same place. It took a couple of weeks to figure out how to prove he was lying, but I did. He did move farther away from their school. The GPS doesn't give exact coordinates. It bounces around between several addresses. I do have a general idea of where my children are when they are with him. It provides some reassurance. My lawyer knows he is withholding his new residency. She emailed his lawyer. His lawyer keeps replying he didn't move. Nothing else is being done. He's been lying to me about his address for months now.

His new home explains why there are so many lates on the kids' report cards. He's not in their school district anymore. He's a forty-minute drive away. On his days, I can track if he gets them to practice and games on time. Sometimes, one of the children leaves their bookbag in his car. I can tell because the GPS travels all over the place. It will be his time to spend with the children, and he is driving everywhere. I know he didn't bring everyone with him. What I don't know is who is watching them. Is it his girlfriend? Is it my oldest? Someone else? I don't know. But when he leaves, he is gone for a long time.

Sometimes he goes to work. He's a general manager, and he likes to say he makes his own schedule. He says he can arrange his time however he wants. The custody schedule is the same every week, and he frequently works on days he has the children. Other times he says he's the manager, and he has no control when he goes in. If an employee calls out, he has to work. I think it's a convenient way to dodge responsibility.

I'm at the final stage of this phase. I go through and rename all the screenshots with the date and sometimes something to identify it at the end. For example, 11.23.24LunchMoneyReceit. Long text messages are numbered separately: 08.14.24-1, 08.14.24-2. The files are already backed up to my Google drive. I pay a yearly subscription for the extra space. Shutterfly is free, and I upload them there as well to a specific album. Last, the files are transferred to the SD card in my phone.

One of my friends had a divorce worse than mine. She kept her documentation on an external hard drive. Her husband was coming into the house while she was gone. She found out from her neighbor, who knew they were getting divorced. He saw her husband go inside several times. She tried to call the police. They couldn't do anything because his name was on the deed and no protection order was in place. She placed cameras inside to monitor while she was gone. The divorce wasn't finalized. But because she had the children almost all the time, she got to live in the house. Of course, he was fighting with her about that. She tried to keep the external hard drive in the car until he stole her license plates. She called the police, but the vehicle was also in his name. He could take the license plate. She became afraid he would also take the car. The hard drive ended up in her purse, and she carried it with her everywhere. That was hers. That was something he couldn't take.

My coffee is gone at this point. Getting comfortable on the couch doesn't stop my body from getting stiff and sore. When the weather cooperates, I take a break for a short walk. It's cold today. I don't consider it an option. I pour another cup of coffee while I cook scrambled eggs and toast. It's a quick ten-minute break before I start the next phase.

I need to be at the table for this part. My personal planner is out, and the custody documentation planner is out. It is easier for me with paper. Switching between screens on my phone was frustrating. I bet there is a simpler way to do this. I've studied videos and listened to podcasts about terrible divorces and documentation tips. Sometimes I find good advice that is free. In fact, I have an entire folder of notes from videos, podcasts, and articles. Sometimes the person wants me to buy their documentation system. I have legal fees and three children. I have subscriptions to three tracking devices. I don't have the extra funds to buy their system. I don't have the mental capacity to research which product will be helpful. I don't have the money to buy and trial-and-error multiple documentation systems. I made my own. It's working okay enough. I streamlined it as I started using it weekly. I should have asked someone to give me a documentation system for my birthday. The one I found would be an expensive birthday gift. If I had the extra money, I would. This has been time-consuming over the last year.

The custody planner is out. The monthly at-a-glance section is filled out with my work schedule, the children's games, practice, and school information. He doesn't share his work schedule with me. It also has the current custody arrangement on it. He cancels sometimes, and that goes on the monthly at-a-glance section, too. Anytime I send him a bill or he pays me, I write it here. It's a quick reference. The details go in the daily planner section. I pull out my phone and jot a quick note on the corresponding day about any communication or information. There are notes about the GPS, if he was late dropping off or picking up a child, or if the children said or did anything strange. The youngest is acting angry toward me. My middle child is more withdrawn. Right now, medical decisions are 50/50, and he is refusing to agree to therapy for them. It's one of the battles I plan to fight in court.

I have found reoccurring themes and color-code things. He is supposed to provide insurance, and he hasn't given me a copy of his card. Every time I ask, it gets highlighted pink in my daily planner. Everything related to money gets highlighted in green. I tried searching through text messages, and it was overwhelming. He sends long messages ripping me apart, accusing me of taking them away from him, and swearing at me. I ask a question that requires a yes or no answer, and he replies with a long tangent stating why he shouldn't have to tell me anything. He accuses me of trying to get back at him. He won't answer the question. Looking back through those texts was too much. If I need information now, I check the planner and find the color coding. If I need to, I go to the date the text was sent for context. The custody planner cuts through the noise, and I can find facts much faster. Some days have more noise than others. Some days we don't text. Those days are wonderful.

I look ahead at my planner to check if there is anything important I need to tell him. I message him when

I make the doctor's appointments. At the beginning of the month, I send another text reminding him about the doctor's appointments for the month. My lawyer says I don't have to give reminders. He doesn't show up anyway, but he likes to say I am trying to push him out of the children's lives. I don't provide reminders of school events. The school sends out the texts or flyers for those. I don't give reminders for games and practices. That is what the coaches and apps are for. It is not my job to be his secretary. It is not my job to make him care about the children. It is simply my job to provide him with information related to the children that he would not have access to on his own. Hell, I don't fight when he cancels or cuts his time short. I say okay, and I take them back. I spent years trying to make him care. He won't.

It's the final part of the documentation. I open my spreadsheet app on my phone. I have three separate spreadsheets now. One is a list of every time I asked him for his insurance card. I plan to request it once a month until I receive it. I update that since I sent another text this week.

I don't need to open the money spreadsheet. He hasn't given me anything recently. He is supposed to pay child support on the first of every month and has thirty days to reimburse me for half of the agreed expenses. I would also have thirty days to reimburse him for the expenses he paid for, but he doesn't pay for anything. Shit, he barely gets them new clothes. The kids come back to me in clothes two or three sizes too small or in bad shape. The money spreadsheet keeps the financial tally for me. I have columns for what he owes me, when it's due, when (if) I receive it, and the total amount owed. I also added a column for whether he communicated he was going to be late. This one has been very useful. I send him the financial recap every month, too. He likes to say he gave me money when he didn't.

The last spreadsheet is a list of violations of the current custody order. We haven't been to court yet. We were required to complete two mediations first. Then, his lawyer canceled the first court day. It was kicked eight months down the line.

Everything is done now. I put all my papers away, grab my headphones, a warm hat and a heavy coat. Some weeks are bad. This process can take a long time. Today was a little easier than most weeks. I turn on some Zen music and go for a walk. I don't care that it's cold outside anymore. The walls remind me of a cage. I want the space.

How the hell do I find time for all of this? I ask myself this every week. It's been challenging sometimes. I wake up early on the weekends before the children are awake, or I stay up after they go to bed. I do one phase at a time throughout the day in small segments. Sometimes I ask the oldest to babysit the other two for an hour, and I try to accomplish as much as possible. Today is their day with their father, and he showed up. I can be a little more "leisurely" about it.

The process makes me think back and wonder why I stayed with him for so long. None of these things are new. I noticed them years ago, but they weren't obviously directed at me or my children. The important word being "obviously". I think back to conversations we had at holidays or at friends' houses and the underhanded comments he made about me. I think back to every time he didn't get what he wanted and how it was someone else's fault. He had no self-accountability then and still doesn't. I think about all the shitty things he said to me. When I told him I was hurt, he called me sensitive, emotional, or selfish. My 'favorite' was I was inconsiderate about how I made him feel. It's more obvious now that I haven't been with him. It's more obvious now that I am clearly the punching bag, clearly the scapegoat.

The process also makes me realize all the work I did to keep the family together. I managed everything. I told him everything. I reminded him of everything. I tried to use a group calendar app, but he never looked at it. I tried a physical calendar in the kitchen and he never looked at it. Every evening was a reminder of who needed to go where the next day. Every day was a reminder to make sure it happened. I planned all the birthday parties and family outings. I bought all the gifts for the children and the parties that they were invited to. I did the grocery shopping, the cooking, and the clothes shopping. I tried so hard to keep everything together as I died inside. I still don't recognize myself in the mirror.

Now I spend my free time and energy documenting for court and researching. I am searching for tips on how to document. I am watching videos about emotional and mental abuse and how to recover. I am researching how to help children caught in divorces like mine. My lawyer tells me my children aren't in immediate harm and there is nothing I can do but document. She tells me that I have to let him fail and that's part of how a case will be built against him. Let the children be left at school. Let them be late. As long as they are not in danger, I have to let things happen. How do I learn to let go and stop preventing damage to my children? How do I manage to find this time to document and research every week?

How the hell do I find the money to pay the retainer and the lawyer? I had enough sense to open a separate bank account that he didn't have access to. I also had a credit card in my name only. It's from back at the beginning when we were dating. The limit is high, so I put the lawyer's retainer on it. He destroyed my credit. I wouldn't be approved for a credit card now even if I tried. I pay it down as often as I can, but on months when he doesn't give me child support, I make only the minimum payment. I have no idea how I will climb out of this hole. I can't ask my parents. My dad is frequently sick and is showing signs of dementia. My mom is taking care of him. My brother is going on two years sober and is starting to make ends meet. He had to dig himself out of his own hole. I guess I will have to dig myself out of mine.

Every week. Every fucking week. Shit, sometimes it's daily. I have to figure out how the hell I will get through this. I have to find a way to find the time. I have to find a way to find the energy. I have to find a way to get the money. I have to find a way not to hate myself for putting myself and my children in this position. I have to find a way to feel fucking awful and move through it without dying in it. I don't always succeed. I often think I am dumb and stupid and naive and a failure and a shell and a sham of a person and a mother. But there is no way in hell I will let him mentally and emotionally beat me down anymore.

The process made me realize something. Somehow, I do find the energy. Somehow, I do find the time. Somehow, I do find the money. Somehow, I do find the information I need. It's not easy, and sometimes I fail a lot before I succeed. But I do eventually find what I need. It made me think. What could I do if I applied myself like this in other areas of my life? What could I accomplish if I took this much time and energy and money and invested it in ME? Not documentation, not researching for court, not a lawyer, and not him. What could I do if I put the same energy into me that I put into keeping my family together when we were married? What could I do if I put the same energy into myself that I put into keeping my children primarily with me at the end of this divorce? It's a revolutionary thought.

I find a way to make things happen. It's rough and

messy and takes a while to streamline. I fail a lot. I make a lot of mistakes. But I think I will start looking into that thought.

What could I do if I put time and energy into myself, and what can I do now to start making that happen?

Sylvia and Beth: Ages 41 and 42

Sylvia made a cup of coffee and put her English muffin with jam on a plate next to her bacon. She added a bowl with blueberries, strawberries, and raspberries, and grabbed a container of yogurt, just in case. She carried everything to the armchair by the window and set it on the small table. After taking a second to curl up with a blanket, she checked the time. Beth's time zone was three hours ahead of her. It was worth calling to check if she was available.

The phone rang twice before Beth's excited voice answered. "Sylvie! I wasn't expecting a call! I thought you would be in a place with no service."

"I was. The town I was rafting in, Ohiopyle, was tiny. I'm so glad I was there in the off-season. Parking would be terrible during prime time. It's in the woods, which made for some amazing hiking! The river runs right next to it, and I can walk to the waterfall in ten minutes taking my sweet time. However, it has shitty cell service. I've been using WhatsApp to talk to Darius. I told Connor I was going away for two weeks and I wasn't going to call him while I was traveling. He didn't like that. I think he is jealous because he thinks I'll talk to Darius and not him. It's true; I will. But this is my time for me. I'm not spending it trying to comfort him every day when we discussed it for months beforehand. I'll text him later today. It's been a few days since I've reached out to him."

"Connor makes sense. It's a new relationship.

Darius has had seventeen years of your antics. Does he still need a lot of reassurance?"

"It's me. After seventeen years, I don't like going a long time without talking to him." Sylvia sullenly said.

"Oh my God, Sylvie! Are you attached to a man?"

"Don't rub it in. I've been attached, and he knows it. It hurts my pride."

"It's good for you."

"He's good for me. It's the strangest thing. He had a difficult time with me being polyamorous in the beginning. It didn't help that I was with two other men besides him. I thought he would be the first to leave. I didn't expect any of the guys I dated to stay, but especially not him and especially not for seventeen years. I didn't expect him to be the one consistently in my life." Sylvia said, amazed. "Beth, he's stood by me through so many breakups and so many breakdowns. We would have periods of monogamy, and I didn't have any thoughts that I was trapped. Shit, sometimes he would find another woman before I found another man. He supported me when I visited Ireland for two months and again three years ago when I stayed in Alaska. That was a terrible time difference. He's never been angry when I go on vacations without him. He is the only guy I can be around nonstop for two weeks. I don't even want to rip my hair out at the end of the two-week vacation. I never saw this coming."

"I am so happy for you! I'm guessing his new girlfriend is working out? She's not causing problems anymore?"

"It took time to adjust, but things are going really well right now. They've been together for almost two years. Personally, I think she's enjoying that I am gone. This is Connor's first time with me on one of my trips. It's almost our one-year anniversary. I guess we will see how he handles this vacation."

"Where do you go next?"

"I'm outside of Gettysburg now. I'll be here for two more nights then head east towards the ocean. Mark and his wife and kids will meet me in New Jersey. We are renting a house for a week."

"New Jersey!? For a week!?"

"Yeah. Crazy, right? New Jersey, of all places. There's a little seaside town called Sea Girt we visited five or six years ago. He only had one child at the time, but I don't think having two will change things much."

"Sylvie, how are you going to handle sharing a house with your brother, his wife, and two small children?" Beth said, bemused.

"I'm going to spend two nights in Philadelphia, then come back. Or I might leave a day earlier. That's how." Sylvia burst into laughter, and Beth joined in. "Mark and I are going to use the time to plan Mom and Bob's ten-year anniversary."

"Are you two close to Bob's children? Are they going to help?"

"We aren't close. We were all in our own lives when they started dating and got married. But it's fun when we are all together. His daughter is going to be more hands-on. She will want to be involved, but she's easygoing and has wonderful ideas. Party planning is not a strength of mine, so I have no problem passing that off to her. It will also need to be child-friendly for all the grandchildren. His son said he'd donate money to help cover expenses. Other than that, all we have to do is tell him when and where to show up."

"Will you invite Connor?"

"Probably not, but Darius is coming. He's been teasing me a lot. I promised to play auntie for one day so Mark and Nicole could go out. Darius thinks that's hilarious. Nicole likes to shop at antique stores and Sea Girt has several. I'll play fun aunt with the kids so she and Mark can go antiquing. Or Mark will stay with the kids, and

I'll be the one stuck going. I'm not sure yet. Regardless, I promised them a day for themselves. I'm also doing one night. They can go out to dinner, take a moonlight walk, whatever other romantic thing they want to do that they can't with children. But it needs to be separated. I'm not watching two kids all day and then the same night. Besides, it gives them two separate dates rather than one huge one. Everyone wins. This will be my last solo vacation for a while."

"Oh? Why?"

"I'm buying a house, Beth."

"Oh, shit!"

"Yeah. It's triggering my anxiety, but I'm going to have my house in the woods. I found two I'm interested in. When I'm back home, I'll make an appointment to tour them if they are still on the market."

"How many bedrooms?"

"Three. And two baths. I'm not sure if Darius and I will ever live together. We've discussed it a couple times over the years. But if we decide to, there will be space for both of us."

"That's a huge step for you." Beth said surprised.

"I'm not saying it will happen. I'm saying I'm buying a house with the possibility it could. And if it doesn't, I'll have a guest room and a room to do whatever I want in. You can visit me if you want to get away!"

"I would love to. It's been years since we've seen each other."

"Fucking life got in the way."

"Right? Abby graduates high school this year. Will just got his license and can start doing more on his own. However, Rebecca is 13. I still have a lot of years left."

"How's Brett been?"

"Better. I look back over the last five years and I do notice a difference. His sister and I were recently talking about it. He yells less often. It's still terrible when he does, but at least it's not as frequent. Rebecca has a better relationship with him than Abby. Will has gotten closer to him, but Abby remembers more since she is older. She holds a grudge against him all the years he was unsupportive. Will remembers, but not as much and is more willing to forgive. Rebecca isn't close to Brett, but she gets along with him the best by far. She wants to go out and do things with him. Well, as much as any thirteen-year-old wants to go out with her parents. Abby refuses. She applied for an out-of-state college and plans on going away as soon as she graduates. Will agrees to do things when Brett asks, but that doesn't happen a lot. It's too little too late. I don't think Brett realizes yet. He may never realize it."

"Do you think you will divorce when the children are gone?"

"I'm not sure. I still have so many years left. I can't think about it. Divorce is still not an option. It's better than it was, but Brett is insecure in general. He projects like he is confident and being a CEO helps maintain the facade. When we fight, he still throws it in my face that I cheated on him. He will go through periods where he looks through my phone and reminds me my decisions are why he doesn't trust me. I hate it. I become depressed for days." She somberly said.

"Beth! It's been ten years since he found out you cheated on him! He's still bringing it up?" Sylvia was stunned.

"It's been about fifteen years."

"No way!! That long? How often does he do that?"

"That's gotten better, too. He brings it up every year or two, when we've had a bad fight. It happened about three months ago. We got into a huge argument about Abby going to an out-of-state college. I support her. I think it's a great idea. He doesn't want her so far away. He doesn't want to pay the tuition difference, and he doesn't want her moving to a different state for the in-state tuition price."

"What has that got to do with you cheating on him fifteen years ago?"

"Nothing, but he finds a way to work it in. This was the first major fight in two years. That's an improvement I will take."

"He didn't find out about Sam, right? It would be bad if he found out about him."

"It would be very bad. He hasn't. He would explode and it would end in divorce. I don't think he would forgive me a second time."

"I'm guessing Sam's wife hasn't found out either?"

"No."

"You two have been seeing each other for a couple years now. You are covering your tracks well."

"It's been almost three years. Sylvie, am I a terrible person for not feeling guilty?" Beth nervously asked.

"I don't think so. You've been married for twenty years. We aren't counting the years you dated beforehand. You've been unhappy most of your marriage. I knew after he found out it was a bad time. You've mentioned he'd bring it up over the years. I didn't realize fifteen years later he'd still rub your face in it. At some point, years ago, it was his responsibility to move past it. If he can't, he should have divorced you. Now you are telling me for twelve years you did everything right, he still didn't trust you, and he still goes through your phone?"

"He checks everything. Not all the time, but enough."

"I mean, if he's going to spend twelve years treating you like shit over a mistake, you might as well have an affair. Even if he's never cheated on you, he's done damage in other ways. He's not innocent in this either. Apparently, it didn't stop him from accusing you even when you were faithful."

"I don't know if he's cheated on me. I've suspected

at times. There were questionable text messages and periods when he would be on his phone a lot, but I never found anything concrete. Sometimes I rationalize my decisions with the same logic. He's already accused me of cheating so much, I might as well cheat. The crazy part is I think Sam is the reason things have been better the last two years. Our fight we had was about Abby. It wasn't about us."

"You've been with Sam for three years though."

"It took a while to create a real connection. We liked each other a lot, but it took time for me to realize he's special. At first, it was something new and exciting. It was a man giving me attention and seeing me as a person. He felt the same way. His marriage was stuck. She was, well still is, so wrapped up in their children. She's an intense helicopter mom and micromanages everything. I think she is trying to live vicariously through her children. Now, he's like my partner. He's evolved to someone that means something more to me."

"I understand. It can take me about a year to figure out a guy myself. When I start a new relationship, I end up seeing him a couple times a month. It can take more time that way to find out if he is a good fit for me."

"We still can't see each other a lot. But he's been my support person and I've been his. It's not easy. His mom got cancer and died. He was a wreck and I couldn't be there for him. It was a hard time for us. Teaching Will to drive was so much harder than teaching Abby. She is focused and attentive. It was smooth and simple. Will's ADHD means he gets distracted by a squirrel, quite literally. Brett doesn't have the patience to teach him or to listen to me vent. Sam has been the one listening, giving me ideas, or making me laugh it off."

"I hope sex with Sam is better than with Brett."

Beth laughed. "It's so much fun. It's so much more intimate. I haven't had this many orgasms in a decade."

"I mean, that will decrease your stress level." Sylvia playfully quipped.

She laughed harder. "Yes. I have more patience after seeing him. That's one reason why I think Sam is helping my marriage. Brett and I were talking last weekend, and he said he's noticed we are fighting less. He thinks I nag him less. He said he enjoys having more space to do things he likes. He thinks this is the best our marriage has ever been."

"That's because Sam is filling your needs."

"Yes. I have someone who will listen to me. I have someone who appreciates me and values me. I have someone that will read excerpts from my romance novels and tell me if he wants to do what's written. Sylvie, I've asked him to read entire books, and he has. Sam loves how I dress. He doesn't think I am dressing up for attention or so men will hit on me. He understands it's something I like. Brett never understood that. He's willing to do activities with me that Brett never has in twenty years. We need to be careful, of course. But we've done it. All Brett has to do is provide and help around the house and with the children. That's it. That's easier now as well. It took a long time, but I got him to agree to a housekeeper twice a month. Rebecca is the only child who needs help, and she has two older siblings. Will is great at entertaining her. Abby understands her responsibility includes helping with homework and occasionally driving Rebecca to practices."

"Are you seriously telling me Brett is the happiest he's ever been because he can do what he wants without caring as much about you and the children?"

"Basically."

"Beth. That's terrible. There is no reason for you to feel guilty."

"I don't. Sometimes it's my lack of guilt that I feel guilty about. Then I remember my husband and I have a calmer relationship. I remember an evening with Sam, or a funny conversation. I remember my children are older and won't need me in a few years. I'm the happiest I've been in years. Sylvie, I love him. I love Sam. But I'm married, so it's wrong, and it's not smart at all. I have no idea how long it will last. But I love him," Beth said passionately.

"Listen girl. I am so happy for you. I don't care what it says about me as a person, either."

"Just please still be here if this ever blows up in my face."

"You and I are forever, Beth."

Background voices came through on the phone. Sylvia caught words and pieced together that Rebecca had been looking for her mom. Beth started a side discussion with her daughter. She reminded her to pack for tennis practice and reviewed a list of items to make sure she had everything. It led to another conversation about Rebecca spending the night at her teammate's house after practice. Beth told her to bring a bag for overnight, too, and she would talk to her friend's mother.

"Sylvie…"

"Yep. I heard Rebecca talking. Duty calls."

"I'm so glad we got this in."

"Me, too. I'll text later and send you pictures."

"We should try to squeeze in another phone call in a couple months."

"I would love that. I'll have updates about the house. You will have updates on Abby's graduation. And while Rebecca is packing for tennis and her friend's house, you need to pack breakfast for yourself. I already know you've only had coffee."

Beth laughed. "You have cameras in my house, I swear you do! I'll pack some things to eat during her practice. Promise. I love you."

"Love you, too."

Sylvia carried her empty plate and cup to the kitchen

and put on water for tea. It was still early in the day and shops were starting to open in Gettysburg. She sent a message to Darius and replied to questions her brother had texted. Her phone rang as the water started to boil. The caller ID flashed Darius's name with a picture of him cooking.

"Hi! I thought you'd be at work."

"Hey Babe. I'm running late. I'm on my way now. I thought it would be easier to call before you got busy. What's on your list today?"

"I'm about to sit down and figure that out. I just got off the phone with Beth. I'm going to check out the shops downtown and go to the National Cemetery and the National Military Park. I need to make my reservation for the ghost walk, too."

"It sounds like you've already figured it out."

"I don't know what restaurant I want to eat at." Sylvia smiled as Darius chuckled.

"Is that a kettle in the background? Are you planning lunch after you just ate breakfast?"

"I finished breakfast a while ago, thank you very much. That's why it's teatime. Once I leave and start my day, I won't stop until after the ghost walk tonight. Most of my sightseeing will be on foot. What's up with you today?"

"I think the new hire is still with me again."

"Is he getting better?"

"There's been improvement. He's not a lost cause like I initially thought, but he does need more training. Ranae wants me to go out with her Friday night. A couple of her girlfriends are going out with their boyfriends. She doesn't want to be the only one without a date."

"Oh. A triple date. That sounds like so much fun." Sylvia added extra sarcasm to her voice as she carried her honey and tea over to the armchair, curling back under the blanket.

Darius burst into laughter. "I can't remember the last

time I went out with other couples."

"You dragged me to Trayvon's house for dinner a few months ago."

"Trayvon doesn't count. You like his wife, and I didn't drag you. I pushed harder than usual because I knew you would have fun once you got there."

"I do like her. I did have fun once I got there." Sylvia sighed. "You're right. That doesn't count. Friday I'm leaving Gettysburg and heading to Jersey. Can I still text when I get to Sea Girt?"

"Of course, Babe."

"It won't be interrupting?"

"I'm going to want to know you got there okay."

"Alright. I'll still text."

"I'm at work now; I have to go. Enjoy your day. If we don't talk tomorrow, I'll call you Saturday."

"Hopefully I'm free. I'm not sure what's going on with Mark or his family yet. I'm gonna show up and find out."

"That's fine, Babe. You haven't seen him in a while. We'll talk at some point. Love you."

"Love you, too."

Cassandra: Age 48

I once read that a person needs at least a year after an abusive relationship to recover. I needed more. It took two years to finalize custody and two more years of going back to court to change it. All of that work. In the end, my ex-husband remarried, moved away, and stopped associating with me and the children. Four years of fighting and he vanished of his own accord. However, all the confidence I developed during the divorce, through the custody fight, and in rebuilding my life after is quickly fading. These dating apps are draining. If finding a relationship online is a war, I am losing battle after battle. I have to find the time to go out. I need to hire a babysitter or convince the oldest child to babysit. Then, there is dressing up and going out with so many other obligations in my head. This does not include coordinating schedules. It is discouraging. I am taking a page from my job and doing virtual dating.

My first virtual date is with Ramon. It is embarrassing to admit, but I'm excited to try it out. I've been texting him for a few days, and he sounds polite. He's younger than I am, but he has a son around the age of my youngest. It began bumpy. I prefer a man who responds the same day I text. Ramon would take almost a day between messages. Eventually, he told me he didn't have the app on his phone. After we exchanged numbers, we started texting regularly. Since text is my primary form of communication, it is the first method to weed out men. First, find out if we can communicate through text. If we can, the second step is a call or video chat. I suggested a video chat, and Ramon agreed. We set up 9 pm on

Tuesday, and he chose the app to use. There are so many messaging and video apps to choose from. It is annoying and overwhelming. Luckily for me, he picked one I already have. I changed out of my work clothes into loose gray yoga pants and an oversize sweater. I wanted to keep it simple. He will like me, or he won't, but I'm not an object to dress up and make pretty for any random guy. I send him a quick text asking if he is available. He responds that he's in his hot tub, but he is.

How the hell am I supposed to respond? What the fuck does that mean? Did he forget about the chat and was already in the hot tub when I messaged? Is he trying to be cool? Is he trying to be sexy? Is this his Tueday night routine? Is this an innuendo or is he forgetful? Why does he think it's smart to use his phone in a hot tub? What if he drops it? What the hell is this shit? I feel my age right now. I feel like a mother. Shit, I sound like a mother.

"If you're relaxing, we can reschedule." I text back. He instantly video calls. He is in a hot tub. This is awkward. "You have a hot tub. Don't drop your phone." What the hell else am I supposed to say?

The date remains incredibly uncomfortable. I am rambling, trying to find something in common. He responds mostly in silence. It's the uncomfortable silence of two people forced to be in a room together. Except we aren't in a room. It's a video date, and it's worse than being in a meeting at work.

He asks what "the rest of me" looks like. The moments when I am grateful for yoga pants and oversized sweaters are few. But this is one of them. I move my camera down to show my outfit. I want to see his reaction.

"That's what you are wearing?" he asks disapprovingly.

"This is what I wear."

At another point in this painful, poor excuse of a

conversation, he states it's old fashioned to talk on the phone. This is not helping my age complex.

"A simple phone call before driving out to meet one man would have saved me a lot of time. And a call to another guy who lived an hour away did save me time. I have three children. It is hard to go out on dates."

"In person is different than over the phone."

"I disagree. Two people who like each other can talk over the phone. You could think of this as saving money. You didn't have to buy dinner. You suffer through this conversation at home sitting in your hot tub."

"Who said I would have bought dinner? I'm a manager at a liquor store. I can get drinks for free from my job," he smugly replies.

"Alcohol makes me sleepy and tired." His game is known. It is all an innuendo. The hot tub, comments on what the rest of me looks like, and alcohol all read "object to fuck". I may be almost fifty, but I'm not stupid.

"Wait. Are you saying you've had bad conversations with a lot of other guys?"

"Yes. And it could have been prevented with a phone call."

"So, it's all these other guys and you. Have you ever thought you were the problem?"

Did he say that out loud? He said that out loud. Very defensively. I have wanted to say that to a few of the men I went out with. Yet here it is used against me. My alarm bells go off, and conversations I've had with my ex-husband fly through my head. "I see. There's no chance it wasn't a good match. You jump directly to it is my fault. Well, if that is the case, I'm okay with that. I think being able to converse is a very low bar. I'm not willing to drop my standards lower."

I hear a kid's voice in the background. Ramon says his son is coming out of the house and he will call me back. I tell him he doesn't need to. This isn't a match.

Even if I am the problem, that doesn't stop me from being correct. This saved me a lot of time, and I didn't have to go through that in person. That was a painful nineteen minutes and sixteen seconds.

✱✱✱

I needed time off after that "date". I decided to keep up the conversations I had already started. No one likes being ghosted. I didn't look for new prospects, and all the 'potential suitors' stalled before a week passed. I began looking again. Reflection over the years helped me realize that having a "type" may be problematic. This time around, I am going to step out of my comfort zone and consider men I usually wouldn't. I swiped on several and matched with a few. Most of the conversations fade into nothingness after two or three days. One man captures my attention.

Patrick is sexy. He is my age and reminds me of a darker Boris Kodjoe. I stare hard at his profile. He is very attractive, but a little farther away than I would prefer. His bio is underdeveloped, but he is an analyst for the government and has a beautiful, clean house. As far as profiles go, this one reads more stable and educated than many others have. He might be able to match me intellectually. In the safety of my mind, I admit I would drive outside my preferred zone for a guy who looked this handsome. I couldn't imagine he would be interested in me.

I scan his pictures and prompt responses looking for flaws. I can't find any immediate red flags. Is an underdeveloped profile a red flag? I haven't decided yet. Does it matter if I don't have a chance in hell with him? I can swipe right and nothing could happen. That would be fine because that's what I expect. But if I swipe left, it is definite nothing will happen. I convince myself to do it. That's why I'm here. To take chances and find someone. I swipe right.

Holy shit, it's a match! I stare at my phone in disbelief. I am surprised at my level of excitement. This must be the dopamine hit researchers talk about. I guess I haven't grown out of having reactive neurotransmitters. I have enough sense to follow up with a message. He responds in a timely fashion, and the back-and-forth starts. He is sending real responses. After months of receiving one-word answers, or waiting all day for a sentence or two, the response is refreshing. He writes a solid paragraph. After a few days of texting, he mentions he is traveling next month. He tries to visit a new country every year. He asks if I travel.

These kinds of men are always tricky for me. The simple answer is I love to travel. Or, more appropriately, I would love to travel. But I'm not able to. My finances are not in line for yearly trips to other countries. It took years to pay off the debt I accrued during the divorce. It's also hard with three children. When a man asks if I travel, is he including the children? Traveling with children is different. I chose the destination, activities, and restaurants with them in mind. I try to do things I think they will like. But sometimes I am wrong. Or they act their age. thirteen- and sixteen-year-olds like to complain about everything. Will my daughter want to come? She will be eighteen and is graduating high school. Do I factor any of them in? How long is someone in a relationship before international travel enters the picture? I don't know. I also have to go around their academic calendar and sports schedule. I can't go away for a long weekend. Is he expecting me to leave my children with someone else while we travel? How will a man who loves exotic trips adapt to my situation? Is this what dating is like? Am I always going to overthink everything? I am already exhausted.

Patrick will not know how deep into the rabbit hole I fell. I keep my answer simple and reply that travel has been hard to do over the last few years with three children. "You should travel," he replies. I glare at my phone. The childless man with a government job says I should travel. What an arrogant asshole.

Despite sounding like a pompous dick, I decide to give him a pass. It is the first warning sign, and it is through text. I ask what he likes to do when he travels. We might have things in common and be able to do similar activities closer to home.

"I like to go to the places in the area that the city doesn't want people to see. I like to go outside the tourist places. I've been to ghettos in Paris where minorities are living in terrible conditions. People think Europe is beautiful and Africa is poor, dirty and filthy. People need to know that isn't always true. I've been to places in the United States that most people wouldn't spend two minutes in. Growing up, I was always around different cultures. Diversity is important to me, and I want to be around someone who appreciates that as well. Travel is education for me. Other than that, I make sure that I try different food wherever I go."

Somehow, I keep ending up in situations where I have no idea how to respond. I went through a terrible divorce and custody battle. I have three teenagers. I have two decades of experience in my field, from several positions and perspectives. How is trying to date leaving me speechless? I do appreciate someone willing to step outside their comfort zone and visit places off the beaten path. I do not think using a ghetto as a tourist destination is the way to do it. It sounds like voluntourism for social media. Again, this is text. He might not actually be pretentious, but this is twice. I decide to change the subject. I ask what he is looking for.

"I've made mistakes with women in the past. I would like to find the right woman to marry and be with for the long term. I've even thought about having a child or two."

My jaw fell. He is forty-eight years old, and he wants to have a child or two. I take a second to acknowledge my judgment and let all my opinions of him run rampant through my mind. Has this man even been around children of any age for any length of time? I respond I don't want to remarry, and I don't want more children. Good luck in your search. And then I unmatch him.

In my sincere effort to give online dating an actual chance, I swipe on Paul. Nothing strikes me about him, but nothing turns me away. He's an average-looking man, albeit maybe awkward. Not the weird awkward. The kind of awkward that might have a sweet heart but not the best social skills. He also has a cat. As I age, I find the ease of a cat simpler than the work required for a dog. Paul seems like a frequently overlooked good guy. He might be a little boring, but after the chaos I've experienced, boring is fine. There are no surprises or excitement when we match.

We start texting, and after two days I realize I still have no anticipation or enthusiasm. It is disappointing since he's pleasant and respectful. He sends daily 'Good morning' and 'Good night' messages. Every afternoon as a variation of 'How is your day?'. I understand many women would love this. It does nothing for me. They are polite gestures, but work meetings and fights with my teenagers are not something I want to share with Paul. I plan to end it, but I don't have the heart. It takes a week before I reach my limit and send him one of my prepared messages. Soon after I started online dating, I realized it was more efficient to have a list of pre-typed responses I could copy and paste. Paul received the "it's not working for me" message.

"We've been talking for a while, but I'm not feeling a connection. You've been respectful, and I didn't want to ghost you, but I think it's best for me to explore other matches."

Most of the men who receive this unmatch me immediately. Paul's response surprises me. "I was just getting ready to ask you if you wanted to go out to dinner. You can't really get to know someone just through texting. But I understand if you want to stop." Paul, who seemed like a nice guy, is acting like a nice guy. I take a few hours to think about it. I've had terrible text conversations. I've had terrible in-person dates. I've had terrible virtual chats. At this stage, what do I have to lose? I send him a message about video chatting, and he agrees. We arrange a time for later that night. He has never used the app before and needed to download it, but still is on time.

"Hi. I was surprised you wanted to video chat with me."

"You are right about texting. Some people converse better talking rather than typing. Besides, the point of doing this is to meet people."

"Exactly. Most people read a text and fill it in with what they think it means. It gets easier after knowing a person, but even then, messages can be misread."

"This is true."

The rest of the conversation is slow, but at least he can converse. Conversations about employment are a common subject on my dates. We end up discussing his job fixing circuit boards. It is as dull as it sounds. There is no spark. I am as disengaged in talking to him as in texting him. I make up an excuse about getting up early to explain my visible yawns. I hold out another ten minutes with small talk, then execute my escape. "I appreciate your time, but I'm going to stand by my original statement. I'm not feeling any connection, but I wish you the best of luck in your search."

"I'm really sorry to hear that. I was hoping you would change your mind. Thanks for talking with me, and I hope you find a match, too."

Paul was worth the video chat. It was refreshing to have a dull date with a guy who seemed like a good guy rather than a bad date with a guy sitting silently in a hot tub. However, dinner, or any meal for that matter, would have been painful. It is official. I am keeping this format. I will text for a couple of days, followed by a video chat or phone call. I have no idea whether this makes me old or young. In fact, online dating makes me feel like I don't have a clue what I am doing. Many of my insecurities I thought I'd resolved in the divorce are making a comeback. This is not part of the plan or a desired result. I spent years rebuilding myself only to have these stupid fucking apps undo my work in six months.

I get up and go to the bathroom, lighting the candles I keep on the sink and turning the lights off. I turn the shower on, allowing time for the water to heat up. I designed it to be relaxing and soothing, including investing in a showerhead that will mimic rainwater. The days of having my children walk in on me sitting on the toilet are long gone. They have a separate bathroom that they are responsible for. This is my master bath attached to my room. This is my little haven. None of my children come in here. This is my treat after years of toys in the tub, pee on the floor and seat, and clogged toilets from too much toilet paper. Those stages were followed by years of hair all over the sink, puddles of water on the floor, and bottles of shampoo, conditioner, and bodywash everywhere.

I step into the shower, breathing in the steam, and start my pep-talk. "This experience is a stress test. That is how I will find areas to improve. Growth is not linear. I may end up going backwards before moving forwards. I am not the woman I was all those years ago. I am not the woman

I was all those years ago." I lean my head against the tile on the wall. "Please don't let me be the woman I was all those years ago."

Beth and Sylvia: Ages 65 and 64

Beth rocked gently on the porch swing, a blanket across her lap, reading her book. Out of the corner of her eye, she caught a quick movement and turned to investigate. Birds chirped on the empty feeder and bounced around the empty bath. She made a mental note to refill both later. The sun was becoming visible through the trees, slowly evaporating the dew and warming her skin. The woods surrounding the property helped impede the intense afternoon sun but managed to block whatever heat the morning sun provided, too. She pulled the hood of her sweatshirt up and wrapped it closer against her. She was used to temperatures in the seventies by this time. The cold made her thin frame shiver, and she considered going inside. Rustling distracted her from watching the birds. Sylvia was coming out of the forest. She was dressed in hiking boots, leggings, and a short-sleeved shirt that displayed the tattoos covering her arms. The birds scattered as Sylvia approached. She looked at the feeder and bath and scowled at them. Then, she headed towards her car, popped the trunk, and grabbed a small bag of bird food to refill the feeder.

Beth laughed. "Sylvie, your age is showing. You picked a house in the woods with a porch swing, and you brought bird seed to a vacation rental. You are an old crone."

Sylvia gave her a side-eye. "Listen woman. You are showing your age. You are wrapped up in a sweater and blanket, reading a physical book. Who the hell owns the physical copy of a book anymore? You are the old lady in the nursing home that's always cold."

"I live in a desert in the south. This is winter weather."

"This is perfect. Besides, crones don't hike in the woods. They stay in their cottage and in the garden. But old ladies sit on porch swings and read."

"You picked this place because it has a porch swing."

"Don't change the subject." Sylvia said in mock indignation. "Did you eat breakfast yet? It doesn't look like it."

"I didn't. Did you go for a hike without eating?"

"No. I had a snack before I left. Breakfast is for after. I'll make us something and bring it out. You mind those old knees of yours and keep reading. Don't forget your readers are on top of your head." Sylvia smirked as she went inside.

Beth laughed, pulling down her glasses. Sylvia walked in and out of the small house. First, filling the bird bath with fresh water and moving tables closer to Beth. Next, she brought out spoons and a plate with buttered toast and two glass cups made into strawberry and banana yogurt parfaits. Last came two cups of hot coffee and a jam jar tucked under her arm.

"I've waited decades for your fig jam. It took entirely too long for us to get together. And for me to try your jam." Sylvia slathered it across her toast as she spoke.

"My fig tree is small but mighty." Beth cautiously sipped her drink and took small bites of the parfait.

"I don't forgive you for sending me photos and never mailing me any."

Beth laughed. "This did take entirely too long to have a girls' weekend."

"Yes. It fucking did. Stupid life. Your children had to go and have babies, and you had to go play grandmother."

"I love it. Being a grandmother is better than being a mother," she said cheerfully.

"A lot of my other friends say that."

"I don't have the pressure to raise them. I don't have to worry about what I'm doing right or wrong. If I can't take them, I simply say no. I don't have to find the time, the energy, or the willpower to make things work. I can take them, have fun, and give them back."

"Be honest with me, Beth. We are in the middle of the woods. No one is close. Does it help that Brett isn't here?"

"Yes. It does," she admitted, hesitantly continuing. "Life felt so much heavier when he was around. It was easier when I was alone and everything was, without question, my responsibility. Being with him and having all the responsibility was a pressing weight on my shoulders. It was a huge burden. I shouldn't have been so alone with someone." Beth paused for a long time, watching the birds. She ate her parfait delicately and sipped coffee between bites. "Sylvie, after the car accident, after he died…" She took a deep breath in. "I cried because I knew I was free. I didn't cry because I was sad. I wasn't. I had been dead for years. I cried because I was free." A tear ran down her face. She turned to Sylvia. "I'm going to burn in hell."

"If whatever higher power is so cruel to send you to hell for that, then I'd want no part of heaven. We'll burn in hell together." Sylvia gazed into space for several moments. "Did you know there's a story about the same situation?"

"No."

"Give me a second. I've gotta dig way back in my memory for this one. It was set in the Victorian era. A woman with a heart condition was told that her husband had been killed in a railroad accident. She cried hysterically, then went to her room alone, where she was overwhelmed with joy that she was free. But her husband ended up walking into their home. There had been a mistake, and it turns out he wasn't dead. But the woman, upon seeing her husband alive, died."

"You are shitty at providing comfort, Sylvie. How has Darius managed to stay with you?" Beth flatly stated.

"The Story of an Hour! That's the name! Her last name was the same as a composer's... Chopin! Kate! Kate Chopin! I knew it would come to me. Fuck you and your old-crone comments from earlier. I'm as sharp as a knife." Sylvia smiled with pride as she drank her coffee and took a large bite of toast. "The point is," she said through the food in her mouth, "you aren't alone, Beth. You aren't the only woman who has had relief when her husband died. I'm sure a lot of women have experienced something similar. I wasn't sad."

"Rebecca took it the worst."

"I'm not surprised. I guess your ability to stay poised and composed at all times came in pretty handy."

"It did. Everyone is so used to my handling shit. The few times I was overwhelmed, people assumed it was because of grief. I didn't correct them. I mean, there was grief. I had a life with him. But I think I was mourning the time I lost, the energy I spent, the dreams I gave up on. I wasn't mourning his death."

"Beth, there is no judgment from me," Sylvia reassured her.

"I know." Beth nibbled her toast, rocking the swing with her feet. She sat silently for several minutes. She found solace in the warm air as the sun climbed over the trees. Country scents drifted in the light breeze. She took a deep breath in and appreciated the notes of pine and honeysuckle. Beth realized her shoulders were tense from the chilly morning and relaxed them down.

"You did it smart, by the way. I've told you before, but I'm gonna tell you again. The way you and Sam planned everything to be able to be out in public was genius."

"I was jealous for years that he divorced his wife. He understood why I didn't divorce Brett. He didn't agree with it, but he didn't throw it in my face. He did remind me that my decisions were keeping our relationship as it was."

"He was right."

"He was. I couldn't argue with him." Beth admitted.

"What do your children think of him now that it's been several years?"

"They still don't have a problem with him. It was wonderful, they never did. I'll never tell them that we had an affair. I'll take that to my grave. Being alone for the first twelve or eighteen months was the best decision I made for myself in a long, long time. Sam supported me one hundred percent. Outside of the bad optics of dating right after my husband's unexpected death, I needed the time and space to be my own person."

"What I remember so clearly was your excitement when you and Sam were planning to meet each other 'for the first time.'"

Beth laughed. "Oh, that was fun! And then going out on dates without caring who saw. I have no idea whether people were fooled. My God! How many years had we been having our affair? Hold on, let me do the math. Twenty! No, Brett died, and we waited. Twenty-one or twenty-two years together at that point. I don't think Brett ever discovered it. He still kept checking my phone, but I don't think he paid close enough attention to me. He had several affairs of his own during that time. I don't think my children realized I was having one, too. Abby left right after high school. Will and Rebecca were still living with us when we found out about one of Brett's side girlfriends. That was my opportunity to divorce him, and I still didn't. I don't know why. I think that is another reason my children liked Sam. He didn't cheat on me. After we were 'dating' for a year, we moved in together." Beth fell silent again. 'I've been so happy these last five years. Why didn't I leave when I had a legitimate reason?"

"Well, at the time, you said it was for the children."

"Rebecca was almost done with high school."

"Your parents have always played a part."

"My father had died."

"Was it financial?"

"No. I had my own accounts and my own credit cards. Some crazy lady told me I should."

"She sounds like a genius." Sylvia saucily said before becoming serious again. "Why did you stay, Beth?"

"I still don't know. To look good? To look like I had it together? To stop him from telling the children about my first affair? Abby wouldn't have cared. Will would have been hurt. Rebecca wasn't born at the time. Probably some sort of fear, I'm sure." she mused.

"I'm sure."

Beth stared off into space. Why did she stay with Brett even after the opportunity to leave presented itself? Beth's wandering thoughts were cut short by dishes clattering and clinking. Sylvia had gotten up and started clearing the table. "Do you want anything while I'm up? More coffee? Tea? Water?"

"I'll take some water."

She nodded and vanished into the house. Beth pulled down her hood and readjusted her blanket. It was one of the biggest questions about her life that she never answered. Why hadn't she divorced him? She thought about college before she met Brett. She thought about her parents' relationship. She thought about middle school and her earliest childhood memories. She didn't hear the front door open and didn't realize Sylvia was back until she handed her a glass. Beth thanked her and took a sip. Sylvia sat down next to her and slowly rocked the swing.

Hot tea was steaming out of the mug she drank coffee from. Beth stared back off into space.

"I think I stayed because staying was easier than acknowledging and facing the truth. I didn't want to deal with the ugly and messy parts. I didn't want the pain. I didn't want the shame or guilt or regret. Change is so hard. No one tells you how much healing hurts. Staying was easier. I knew what to expect. Maybe I believed I didn't deserve better anyway." She paused. "Do you remember the football game we went to when we were in middle school? The one where Ryan and I started dating?"

"I do. I've thought about it several times." Sylvia reflected. "I think at twelve I was polyamorous and didn't realize it. Who realizes that at twelve? The idea wasn't mainstream, or even discussed in public either. I liked Chris and Dylan and loved when you invited me to things. I got to hang out with them. The three of us always ended up next to each other. I remember thinking I should have been jealous when Chris got a girlfriend. I wasn't. She sat next to him and I still sat in between both of them. I never liked Ryan, but when you two broke up, I didn't hang out with Chris and Dylan again. That hurt a lot." She paused. "Now that I think about it, that might have been my first heartbreak. You dated Ryan for about a year, and I wanted them to keep wanting me around after you two broke up." Sylvia rocked the swing and sipped her tea.

"He raped me." Beth simply stated.

She stopped rocking. "I knew something happened."

"I know you did."

"That's why I was adamant we walk home."

"I remember." She stared down at the porch, looking up only when a bird landed in the feeder. She took small sips of water periodically across the long span of silence. Sylvia started to rock again. Beth timed the gentle rhythm to her inhales and exhales. "We did use a side door to get inside the school," she began matter-of-factly. "But we started making out. He started rubbing my breasts. I pushed his hands away but wanted to keep making out with him. He did it again. I told him it was too soon, and we had to go back. I went to the bathroom and as we were walking back to the side door, he asked to kiss me a little more. Of course, I was happy he wanted more kissing. I was happy he was giving me so much attention."

"He pulled me under a stair well and we started making out again. He said something about not being able to feel anything through that big jacket of mine and unzipped it. I told him no. It was too soon. But he said I was pretty and he couldn't help himself. He said all of his other girlfriends let him do this on the first date and I would like it. His hand went up my shirt. I tried to push him away, but he was stronger and taller than me. He said he had something else that I'd like. He unzipped my pants and put his fingers in me. He kissed me so hard the back of my head was shoved against the wall. He pinned my entire body. He said he could tell I liked it because I was wet and he was going to make me feel good."

"I froze Sylvie. I couldn't move. But we heard the janitor. He was listening to the radio. I guess he listened to music while he cleaned. Makes sense. He was supposed to be alone in the school. Ryan said we had to leave before he caught us, grabbed my hand and pulled me outside. He told me to fix my clothes before someone saw me. That he was the only one who was going to see anything. He said I was lucky he chose me because any girl in his grade would love to be in my shoes right now."

Beth took a small sip of water. "I don't think it was technically rape. My therapist says that I am hiding behind semantics. That technicality is irrelevant," she said, detached. "But, he did technically rape me later in the relationship. Not the first time we had sex. Well, the first time I agreed because he threatened to break up with me if I didn't. But there were a couple times I said no, and he didn't listen. In the end, he still broke up with me. Afterwards, I didn't say no to my boyfriends. I just had sex with them when they asked."

"You didn't have many boyfriends in middle or high school."

"No. I knew I wasn't going to say no, so I didn't date a lot. I didn't get any better at picking guys. Before I met Brett, I dated Rob. Do you remember him?"

"Yeah. The soccer player. He was in a frat, too."

"Yes. His frat was close to my sorority. His roommate was in the same fraternity as him. He walked in on us having sex. I panicked and hid under the blankets. Rob laughed and told me not to hide. He said he already saw, and we weren't going to stop just because he was there. He pulled the covers off me and kept going while his friend watched. They were laughing about it. He would tell him to do something to me and Rob would do it. That was the first time I had anal sex. We broke up soon after that. Then I met Brett."

"I didn't know any of this."

"I know."

"Brett makes so much more sense," Sylvia said in quiet thoughtfulness.

"He wasn't obviously abusive. His variety took longer for me to realize. He came from a wealthy family and was going into business. Of course, that was enough for my mom to like him and push me to marry him. I liked his family. I still do. I still visit my sister-in-law and her children. He wasn't bad, or that's what I thought at the time. He was going to be able to provide. I was going to have stability. I didn't think I was going to find anyone better."

"Did you tell Brett any part of what you told me?"

"No."

"Did you tell Sam?"

"Yes. He knows all of it. Everything before Brett. Everything with Brett. All of it. Living with Sam is nothing like living with Brett. Sam is so helpful and considerate. He understands me so well. It took time adjusting to seeing each other all the time. We spent over twenty years with limited contact. But it's easier to address conflict with him. It's not going to be used against me. He's going to listen. If he says he's going to work on something, he actually does. It doesn't matter if it's something simple like taking the car for an oil change or something important like not talking to me when I work from home. He follows through. It's amazing."

"Beth, I am so happy you have that now. I was already happy for you; I'm just happier."

"You aren't angry that I hid those things from you? You are my best friend. You should know everything about me."

"It's your story to tell. God, I wish you told me sooner. But it's not my place to decide who you tell and when."

"Sam asked me to go to therapy when we started dating. Not during our affair, but when we were publicly dating."

"It was smart of him to ask and smart of you to listen."

"I love him, Sylvie. I didn't want to bring all of that into our real relationship."

"It was real when it was an affair, Beth. You were together for over twenty years. It doesn't matter if you couldn't be with him in public or talk to him when you wanted. You both still had to find a way to make it work for over twenty years."

"It's a different real now. Seeing him every day and living with him is very, very real. It's been a lot to adjust to. It's more opportunity for my past to impact my present."

"Absolutely."

"I went to therapy every other week for a year. Whenever I mentioned it, people assumed it was to help me with the grief of losing my husband. That always made me laugh inside. I don't need to go as often now. Only once a month. I think going to therapy is why I can finally tell you. I couldn't tell you when I wasn't even honest with myself."

"Makes sense. I think I am having a hard time right now being honest with myself. I am not adjusting to living with someone I had limited contact with as gracefully and thoroughly as you are."

Beth chuckled. "Is anyone surprised by this, Sylvie?"

"I am! I thought I would be better!" Sylvia talked loudly over Beth's laughter. "No! I thought about all the places I've been and people I've been around and all the adapting I've had to do. I thought I could do it!"

"You are still living with Darius, right?"

"I am. It's been three years Beth! Three!" Sylvia shoved three fingers into Beth's face. "I still have to run away on trips without him. He is not surprised I'm having a hard time. He is taking everything in stride."

"He kind of has to."

"He doesn't have to. But it's in his best interest." It was Sylvia's turn to be silent. Beth gave her the same respect and waited. "I didn't handle it well. When he had his heart attack. I mean, I did. He called me and told me what was happening before he called an ambulance. I was able to meet him at the hospital. He spent the night, had a procedure to fix his heart, spent another night, and was sent home. It could have been worse. He stayed with me for a couple of nights afterwards. I told him he had to. I waited until he was back at his place before I broke apart. I didn't think it was appropriate for me to become hysterical after he was the one just hospitalized."

"I think it's perfectly legitimate for you to be

emotional when Darius could have died."

"Yes, but I wanted to be his support system at that moment. I didn't want him to have to be mine. It took me a year to convince him to move into my house. Do you see the irony here, Beth? I had to convince him it might be better to live together as we got older. I never imagined I would say anything like that! It's my idea. I pushed for it. And I'm still having a hard time."

"Are you two fighting a lot?"

"No. Everything is wonderful. We have our own bedrooms and our own full bathrooms. He's been doing things to stay active and healthy and he's working part time. I have my job and my projects. I love coming home to him. We do go on vacations together. But I still have to go off on my own."

"Why does it mean you are having a hard time because you like to travel alone? What's wrong with that? Does it bother Darius?"

"No. Sometimes I think I'm weird because I don't want to share a room with him. Or a bathroom. And it's weird I still want to travel alone."

"Sylvie. You are weird. You've always been weird. Why would you be normal now that you are sixty-four?" Beth said with endearment. "Does it bother Darius that you two don't sleep together?"

"No. He likes to fall asleep with the TV on. I don't want a TV in my room."

"How are you two navigating your other partners?"

"We've decided to give monogamy a try."

"What! You haven't mentioned another guy or that he had another girl, but I assumed there was no one important. I didn't think there was no one else! Was this intentional?"

"Yes. It was part of the discussion when we talked about cohabitating. How were we going to navigate other partners? Were we going to agree on our metamours coming into our shared space? Did we want to adjust to living together and be considerate of them as we learned to cohabitate? In the end, we decided to be monogamous for a year as we adjusted. But after a year, I didn't want to find another partner. He didn't either. We are in our sixties. We've done this for over thirty years. Right now, we are good and don't want to date other people. The door is always open. We have a standing agreement to keep an open conversation about it. But I don't have the bandwidth. This monogamy thing and living together takes up a lot of time. It's fucking hard! How did you do this for years, take only two and a half years off, then do it again?" Sylvia exclaimed, perplexed. "How Beth?"

"Sylvie, I have no idea how you spent decades handling all of your partners and all of Darius's partners," she responded, amused by Sylvia's antics.

"Oh, that wasn't hard once the initial infatuation phase passed. Well, never mind. Some metamours made it easier than others. But this monogamy thing is tricky. Sometimes I feel guilty we have separate rooms and sometimes going to my own space and closing the door is how I stay sane."

"I loved going to bed before Brett. It was my alone time. He would be in the living room watching TV, then come into the bedroom and turn that one on. Sometimes it would wake me up. I would have loved to have my own room. Sam knows my opinions on it. It's one of our compromises. We designed an extra room for his own space and in return there is no TV in our bedroom."

"That's a fair trade off."

"It works for us. And separate bedrooms works for you. Don't be so hard on yourself. What matters most is that you and Darius are okay with the relationship. Non-monogamy worked for years and he grew into it. Now monogamy works. You might grow into it." Beth said optimistically.

"I might. I don't want to take the time to find a new partner and figure out if he will work or not. I'd rather appreciate my current relationships. Mark and Nicole have grandchildren. I am an amazing aunt! I love going to visit them. I'm hoping you and I can make this a normal event. Next year, you can pick. If I have to die in the heat for you, then so be it!"

"You are dramatic. You won't die in the heat."

"You can. It's called heat stroke and happens when it's triple digits outside."

"There will be a pool, Sylvie. I will make sure you don't die."

"We could do a couples' thing! You and Sam and Darius and I."

"I love that idea!"

"We aren't getting younger, Beth. That's another reason why I wanted to live with him. The body starts to go as we age. I have a huge support system. I have things in place where I could be alone. I would be happy and still have a great life. I just think I will have a better life if he's with me."

"Take it from me. Take a risk and go for what you think will make you happier. There is no certificate from the universe saying you get a gold star for doing what everyone else expects of you. You will have a hard time. People who want to marry and live together have periods when it's difficult. You never wanted to live with someone and now you are. It will be challenging. Be kind to yourself. Are you going to get married?"

"No. We discussed that. We considered it for our forty-year anniversary. Instead, we updated our wills and our paperwork to make sure the other person was taken care of. Are you going to marry Sam?"

"Yes. We are talking about it. I think next year. It will be small and simple. His children, my children, a few close friends and his siblings. You and Darius of course."

"Of course."

"And if either of you have a partner you want to bring, you can."

"I don't see that happening. When it comes to dating right now, I am feeling my age."

"Do you remember the account you told me to start the first time I had an affair?"Beth asked.

"Yeah."

"I'm using some of the money for our honeymoon. I never stopped putting funds into it."

"I can't think of a better use for it."

They both fell silent. Several minutes passed before the warmth of Sylvie's arm wrapped around Beth's shoulders. She leaned against her and started rocking the swing again. It felt like another chain had been broken. Beth had been hiding parts of her from Sylvia for decades. With another weight gone, she reached a new level of freedom that she didn't think was possible.

That had been a surprising discovery over the last seven years since Brett's death. Freedom came in pieces and fragments. Beth thought the end of their relationship would be simply that. She thought it wasn't feasible to gain more freedom than knowing someone was dead. She was wrong. Every time Sam caught her, she felt freer. Every time she was with her grandchildren and realized how different she was from her mother, she felt freer. Every time Abby's and Rebecca's husbands, or Will's wife treated her children well, she felt freer. Now she was in a vacation rental for a long weekend with her best friend of almost sixty years. She had no idea how Sylvia loved her through everything. She suspected Sylvia often wondered how Beth loved her through it all, too.

"Sylvie. We aren't going to stay hiding in a house in the woods. If you wanted to do that, you could have stayed home. There's a town about forty-five minutes from here. We are going to see what's there. I'm going to get dressed."

"That's fine. But you aren't expecting me to be as dolled up as you, right?"

"No. Of course not. But I am expecting you to pick out where we are eating for lunch."

Cassandra: Age 65

I am sitting at my desk, watching the storm. The weather is so angry that it is rumbling and roaring. The rain is ruthlessly bashing the pavement. This is an appropriate end to my day of back-to-back meetings. In person. Online. Over the phone. Meeting after meeting after meeting. Today was a day to test my professionalism.

I had two meetings with Bill, the man who should retire but hasn't. He loves to give backhanded compliments. One was led by a recently hired young woman, Amira. I've met her a couple of times, and she has a lot of potential. But right now, she's trying to accommodate everyone. I think she will develop a spine once she is more comfortable. Wendy was there, too. She is a middle-aged woman, younger than me but older than Amira, who likes to criticize everything. A meeting that had Bill also featured an out-of-town client, Donnie. He expects red-carpet treatment when he's here. I had a phone call with Roy, who doesn't stop talking and asks invasive questions. Luckily, I had to follow-up with Kevin, a lovely man who has been a long-time client. He is always pleasant to work with. I still had to attend my regular online meeting. It runs well enough most days. There are two women and a man whom I enjoy collaborating with. Two other men in the group always talk over us. We are used to it and have developed a system, but egos ran high.

There were many moments throughout the day when I took a sip of water simply to make sure my face wouldn't show my real emotions. Drinking water seemed smarter than biting my tongue. I also had to use my dumpster-fire stress ball. My daughter gave it to me years ago. It was supposed to sit on my desk as a decoration. Not today. I put a smile on my face for the camera. I put a smile in my voice for the phone. And I squeezed the dumpster-fire stress ball under the table. Today felt like menopause did. I thought I was past this.

Lunch consisted of taking bites between meetings and bathroom breaks. I talked more than had I wanted to. It made my throat dry and increased the amount of water I consumed. I hate these days. It meant I couldn't complete real work. I stayed an hour late to catch up on items I couldn't put off. I had planned to stay thirty minutes, but the weather decided otherwise. The dark storm clouds that formed throughout the day opted to explode as I was about to leave. I can relate to their pain. The plan was to keep working until the rain eased up. Storms like this often end quickly. I worked an additional half hour. No change outside. I have been sitting at my desk watching the storm for the last ten minutes. I've had enough. I want to go home.

Of course, I didn't pack an umbrella. It was a beautiful morning when I drove in. I was dismayed to discover that I was trapped in meetings on a gorgeous day. As the weather became oppressive, chilly, and dark, I attempted to convince myself this was better. I wasn't missing a pretty day because of work. Except now I am leaving the office late in flat dress sandals, a skirt, and a cream blouse with no umbrella in a torrential downpour complete with thunder, lightning, and a bad parking spot. Out-of-town clients stole the close parking spots. I had to park farther away. By the time I reach my car, my clothes are saturated and clinging to me. My hair is plastered to my head.

The ride home is no better. My shirt is transparent.

The car seat is soaking wet from my clothes and body. I turn on the heat to try to dry them off, but it's making my windows foggy. I don't understand why, and I can't take the effort to figure it out. I alternate between having heat and seeing. I have to pay attention to the road. Everyone is driving at a snail's pace and hitting the brakes. Some of it is appropriate. Visibility with the rain is impaired, and rain is pouring down faster than it can run off or drain. The cars are splashing water on my windshield, and my wipers can barely keep up. It is still not appropriate to drive thirty mph when the speed limit is fifty-five. It is also not appropriate for the car in the passing lane to drive thirty-five mph. This is overkill and making my commute take twice as long as normal.

It is still raining when I arrive home an hour after I left the office. I am two hours behind my normal routine. The front half of my clothes are partially dry, but the back part is still wet. My shoulders are sore from hunching over the wheel. My stomach is rumbling, and my bladder is starting to yell at me. The plan is to run into the house as fast as I can. Except I didn't realize I parked in a puddle. Then, I didn't realize the water running down the street had a current. A strong one. My sandal slips off my foot, forcing me to chase it. It doesn't go far, but I don't bother to put it back on. The step onto the curb proves deceptively treacherous. Traction on dress sandals is nonexistent. It leads to an intimate meeting between my body and the muddy grass. The other sandal falls off and is taken away by the street current. It gets farther this time. I have to pick myself up off the ground. Once I catch it, I run to my house. I spent years getting in shape. In fact, it is a source of internal confidence that I became stronger as I grew older. Rain, a street current, and a curb ripped my pride to shreds in less than five minutes. I wonder what the neighbors saw.

Another reason for running is I have to pee. Three children and a sixty-five-year-old body means that sometimes a sneeze or cough can be dangerous. It doesn't matter how many Kegel exercises I do. I check my purse, and it's closed. Of course it's closed. Nothing fell out when I slipped. I didn't put my keys in my purse when I left the car. I kept them in my hand to get inside faster. Where are my keys? I run to my car, and they are lying in the sodden grass. I rush back, still carrying my sandals and my purse. My hands are dirty and slimy. My keys are muddy and gritty. It has never been so difficult to open a lock, but I manage. I bolt inside, slam the door, and drop everything. I take off running, only to abruptly have an intimate meeting with the floor. I hear my cat yowl and scurry away, briefly registering her fur on my ankle. The next thing I register is the replacement of the cold and wet feeling everywhere with a warm and wet pooling in my crotch. My bladder did not like this impact.

I lean back onto my knees, but I can't pick my forehead off the floor. My hands don't know what to do with themselves. They are in my hair, pulling it. They are fists hitting the hardwood. They are wrapped around my shoulders trying to hug me, then back to pulling my hair and hitting the floor. Small sobs escape. I try to breathe, but I can't. There is too much pressure in my chest. My heart is beating too fast. It's pounding in my ears. My stomach is in knots. I pound the floor so hard that I sit up on my knees. I take a deep breath in, but there is no exhale. There is a long, guttural scream from my soul. The pressure in my chest lessens. The flipping and clenching in my stomach slows. My lungs pull in another deep breath. My hands don't relax. They stay clenched in fists and punch the hardwood, forcefully sending my head back down. Another scream rips. With each pound, another roar escapes. I give in to it and drown in rage. I hit the floor hard.

"Fuck!   Fuck!   FUCK!!   FUCK!! FUUUUUUUCCCCCCCCKKKK!!!!!!!!!!!!!!"

My legs propel me up. The tension in my chest is starting to increase again. My hands grab the nearest item, a vase of flowers on a table, and throw it against the wall. Another scream. My abdomen is tight and my throat is raw, but this scream keeps coming. When it subsides, my breathing is heavy and my body weak. It brings me back to my knees. Slowly, I catch my breath, and my body lowers itself to its side, curling up in a ball.

The tears start. They pour down my face while my body shakes uncontrollably. My hands wrap around my shoulders and squeeze. Snot drips from my nose. The roar shifts to sobs. It's still hard to breathe. The rapid inhales I sneak in between blubbering don't fill my lungs, and my chest is still tight. However, my body has decided it doesn't have to punish everything around it. It has decided that lying here and shaking is enough.

I don't know how long I lay on the floor. Eventually, the sobs subside and change to stuttered, hiccup breathing. Tears stop pouring. They stream, then trickle. My heart decides a regular pace is sufficient. It doesn't need to pound. My stomach decides to untie the knots. Frenzied flipping is no longer required. My lungs decide I can be in charge again. I intentionally breathe air in and out. My chest rises and falls instead of shakes. My hands decide the fight is over. They allow me to open and close them. Harvey, the cat, decides he should check on me and nuzzles his head against my face.

I sit up and assess my hall. The hardwood near the door is wet and muddy. My clothes are covered in mud, grass, and piss. Against the base of the damp wall lay crumpled and broken flowers. Large chunks of glass rest in a pool of water. Glass shards and water spray are scattered like a Jackson Pollock painting across the hall. After checking to make sure no glass reached me, I cautiously stand. I take off my blouse and bra and drop them to the side. I stand and slip off my skirt and underwear, dropping them into the pile. I contemplate drying my feet on the doormat but decide against it. At this stage, dirty footprints are the easiest things to clean up.

I walk upstairs to my room, find sweatpants and a tee shirt, then head to my bathroom. I light my candles and let the shower water run until it is warm. I step inside, and the warmth pours over me. After a few minutes, my body adjusts, and I increase the temperature. I grab my loofah and wash, repeating the action because it's soothing. After shampooing and conditioning my hair, I open my sugar scrub. I use it on special occasions. I don't know if what happened could be classified as a special occasion, but I'm going to use it, anyway. I take my time, breathing in the lovely vanilla lavender scent, then step out of the shower.

After sliding into comfy clothes, I head downstairs, bypass the mess, and head for the kitchen. I reheat leftovers and take out a big wine glass and a bottle of wine. Everything is placed on my dining room table. The quiet sounds beautiful after the hours of meetings, the traffic on the way home, and whatever the fuck happened in the hall. I take my time and enjoy my food and drink and then take everything to the kitchen. It is only me in the house, besides Harvey. I don't use enough dishes to run the dishwasher. Most of the time it is faster to handwash. I don't wash the wine glass; I refill it. I start with the easiest task. I mop the footprints to my room and bring my laundry down. My destroyed outfit gets tossed in with my other clothes in the laundry hamper. I'm curious as to whether it will end up clean.

I head back to the hall and stare at the piss and mud

on the floor. It felt like decades of rage had exploded from my body and soul. Where the hell did all that anger come from? I think about it as I mop. There was my marriage and my divorce. I thought I did okay with that. Afterwards, I went to therapy and found therapists for my children, too. My ex stayed an asshole throughout his intermittent involvement in their lives. I got braver as they got older. But there was so much I wanted to say that I didn't, that I couldn't. It would escalate him. He would want to be more involved to prove me wrong. But if I stayed quiet, he would vanish on his own.

I resisted the urge to call him an irresponsible, lazy, selfish piece of shit. I resisted the urge to call him a lying, manipulative, fuckface. I resisted the urge to call him out every time he canceled his time. Every time he said he would give me money, and didn't. Every time he wanted me to play secretary. Every time he said he'd changed, and he still loved me. Every fucking time I resisted. Years of silence. Years of taking the high road. Years of simply saying 'Okay.'

I did take the same resources I used for the marriage and for the divorce and use them for myself. I started going to the gym. Over the years I've done swimming, Pilates, weight lifting, and marathons. I made friends at work. The children got older, and I could go out for a couple of hours with colleagues. I didn't pay as close attention to the custody order. He never did follow it. But I never stopped documenting. It became easier as he was less involved. My children were with me almost full time because he canceled all the time. I took my career in a new direction and excelled in it. A salary increase followed. That was a huge help. He still owes tens of thousands of dollars in back child support. I took them on long weekend trips, got them cars when they turned sixteen, and provided a stable life for them. All three are doing well now. I restarted hobbies I had when I was younger and read books for fun. I thought I had bounced back exceptionally well.

While I refill my wine, I check out the floor and analyze the next step. I shouldn't be barefoot if I'm going to clean up glass. I slide on a pair of flip-flops. It's not the best choice, but it's better than slicing my flesh on glass. Since the hardwood is still wet, sweeping won't work. I decide to use my mop instead. My mind wanders as I collect and pile shards of glass.

I bit my tongue a lot while I was dating, too. I tried dating on and off for years. Many times, I resisted saying I could take a joke, but what he said wasn't funny. Especially when it was at my expense. Many times, I resisted saying my children's father was not his business. He didn't need to ask, "What about the father?" I wasn't asking him to parent my children. Many times, I resisted telling a guy he was acting like a fucking entitled dickhead. I did find a couple of guys. We would date for a year or two, but it stopped working and we would break up. The last boyfriend I had was five or six years ago.

I have realized I am happier alone. I enjoy coming home to Harvey. I enjoy choosing what to watch, or listen to, or being in silence. I enjoy taking trips to visit my children and grandchildren whenever I want. I love that I don't have to discuss any plans with a partner like my friends do. I have no children to raise. I have no husband or boyfriend. I have seniority in my job. It gives me more freedom than most. After decades of being responsible for everything and everyone, the peace that comes with solitude has been priceless. I've considered something easy and fun with a man. I might have another twenty years in me, and I might not want to be alone for all of it. But right now, being alone is fucking amazing.

The water is mopped up, and the debris is piled

together. I bring my garbage bin over and start with the flowers and large shards. I'm expecting the glass to cut me. That would match the energy of the day. I'm anticipating little glass splinters to utilize guerrilla warfare on me the rest of the week. Some small slivers always manage to hide until the bottom of my foot finds them. It surprises the fuck out of me when I clean everything up without getting stabbed or sliced. Blood is not on the list of fluids that expel from my body today. Wine needs to be refilled. The laundry needs to be switched. Dessert needs to be eaten.

I congratulate myself on my earlier decision to find a wine that pairs with chocolate cake. It is a decision I am proud of. Except I didn't plan on finishing the bottle in one night. I planned on a couple of nights of wine and chocolate cake. Best laid plans, I guess. I will have one night of wine and a couple of days of chocolate cake. Never mind. I am going to repeat a successful decision. I will have to buy another bottle of wine that pairs with chocolate cake. That will be my mission for tomorrow. Never mind. Change of plans. I grab my phone and start researching wine that pairs with chocolate cake as I eat my cake.

Midway through dessert, it hits me how ironic my situation is. I am a woman of action in a position of leadership. It is my job to address problems and accomplish goals. Yet I have silenced myself so many goddamn times. I would love to tell the two men in my regular Zoom meeting that what they said isn't original. If they shut their goddamn mouths long enough to listen, they would realize one of the women in the group had already said it. *Stop fucking interrupting.*

I would love to tell Roy to fuck off when he asks questions he has no business asking. I would love to tell Wendy to critique her fucking self before she acts like a supercilious bitch. That would be amazing to say. Does she know what that means? The look on her face would be priceless. And whenever Donnie is in town, I'd love to tell him to pull his head out of his fucking ass. The secretary is not a server or caterer. She is busy managing the details in the background for things to happen smoothly. And if I hear one more goddamn time about how much business he brings, I may break a glass vase over his head instead of against a wall. Maybe, just maybe, I'll give Bill a backhanded compliment in return and then tell him to fucking retire. Fuck. I am sixty-five. Why do I have to play these childish games?

My piece of cake is finished. The wine is gone. Everything is cleaned up. Now what the hell am I supposed to do? Where's the guidebook for pissing on yourself in an anxiety attack? Was it an anxiety attack? A rage attack? I guess after I find the guidebook, I'll have to flip to the index, check under all the synonyms for pissing, and start there.

I make my way upstairs. That takes more time than I thought it would. I haven't drank this much in years. I don't remember how to walk drunk. I avoided cutting myself while cleaning. Now I need to avoid a concussion from falling backwards down the stairs. I manage, but it's probably because Harvey is already curled up on my bed and can't trip me. Tomorrow's goal, and for the rest of the week, will be not stepping on glass.

I flop onto the bed. Harvey jumps up and runs away. It serves him right. We are even now. I turn the music on my phone. I normally sleep in silence, but now it's been quiet for too long. I don't remember the last time I was drunk. I think I will lie here and relax. I think that is a great next step. Over the weekend, I'll go to the dispensary across town and buy marijuana. I haven't smoked marijuana before. I haven't smoked anything. I've heard about pot drinks and pot gummies. Gummies sound good. It is very apparent that I am too composed. I am wound too tight. I am sixty-five. I am financially stable. My children are gone. I have no one to answer to. What the fuck do I really have left to prove? Tomorrow I will make a list of things to do that I am not supposed to do and start fucking doing them any goddamn way.

About the Author

Mae Andrews is originally from Upstate New York but currently resides in the Mid-Atlantic region. In her first life, she majored in English and minored in Women's and Minorities Studies and is currently transitioning to her third life as an author. She is a single mother to an amazing teenage son.

Her spare time is spent listening to podcasts, watching YouTube, going for walks, navigating her son's sports games and practices, and snuggling with her cat.

Check out her website:

Check out her social media:

maeandrewsbooks

www.ingramcontent.com/pod-product-compliance
Lightning Source LLC
Chambersburg PA
CBHW060433130626
46555CB00005B/2332